"You D[...]
But [...]
A Boy Should Know His Father."

That was a low blow, one that blew past her anger and went straight for her heartstrings. Who would she be hurting if she fought to keep Bear from Nick? Sure, she could exact some revenge for Nick's repeated abandonment of her. But in the long run, it was Bear who would suffer. Would she really do that to her son?

Could she really do that to Nick?

As if he could feel that the attention of the adults had shifted away from him, Bear began to get upset. Tanya took a step toward him, but Nick put a hand on her shoulder. "I got him," he said, a peaceful smile on his face.

Tanya watched as the man of her dreams swooped her son up into a big hug and then grabbed a book and settled down to read him a story. Tears swam across her vision.

She couldn't keep Bear from Nick. She just couldn't.

But what would letting Nick back into her life do to her?

Dear Reader,

Welcome back to the Red Creek Lakota Reservation! This time, a new set of challenges faces the Red Creek Lakota. Rosebud Armstrong has hired Nick Longhair to come back to the reservation and lead a case against a natural-gas company that may have polluted the groundwater.

Nick's a native son of the tribe who went off to law school and never came back. He's made quite a name—and fortune—for himself as an environmental lawyer. He's not exactly thrilled about being back home. The reservation is a reminder of the poverty he left behind.

Poverty wasn't the only thing he left behind. His childhood sweetheart, Tanya Rattling Blanket, is the only bright spot he has to look forward to. The last time he saw her was two years ago. He's hoping to pick up where he left off, but Tanya has other plans.

Tanya's changed, in more ways than Nick can imagine. When he meets her baby boy, Nick finds himself wondering if he'll ever be able to leave the reservation again. Will Nick turn his back on the love of his life—and the family he always wanted—to keep chasing his dreams of wealth and power?

A Man of Distinction is a sexy story of coming home and finding yourself. I hope you enjoy reading it as much as I enjoyed writing it! Be sure to stop by www.sarahmanderson.com, and join me when I say, long live cowboys!

Sarah

SARAH M. ANDERSON

A MAN OF DISTINCTION

HARLEQUIN®

entertain, enrich, inspire™

Recycling programs
for this product may
not exist in your area.

ISBN-13: 978-0-373-73197-8

A MAN OF DISTINCTION

Copyright © 2012 by Sarah M. Anderson

www.Harlequin.com

Printed in U.S.A.

Books by Sarah M. Anderson

Harlequin Desire

A Man of His Word #2130
A Man of Privilege #2171
A Man of Distinction #2184

SARAH M. ANDERSON

Award-winning author Sarah M. Anderson may live east of the Mississippi River, but her heart lies out west on the Great Plains. With a lifelong love of horses and two history teachers for parents, she had plenty of encouragement to learn everything she could about the tribes of the Great Plains.

When she started writing, it wasn't long before her characters found themselves out in South Dakota among the Lakota Sioux. She loves to put people from two different worlds into new situations and see how their backgrounds and cultures take them someplace they never thought they'd go.

When not helping out at school or walking her two rescue dogs, Sarah spends her days having conversations with imaginary cowboys and American Indians, all of which is surprisingly well tolerated by her wonderful husband and son. Readers can find out more about Sarah's love of cowboys and Indians at www.sarahmanderson.com.

To Jason, for being my hero as a father and husband.

One

Nick Longhair got out of his Jaguar, his Italian loafers crunching on the white rock that made up the parking lot at tribal headquarters for the Red Creek Lakota. The building might have had a fresh coat of paint in the past two years, but otherwise, it was as he remembered it. Narrow little windows, low ceilings and an overall depressing vibe.

For the past two years, he'd worked out of a corner office on South Dearborn, one of the priciest blocks in Chicago. Marble floors, custom furnishings and floor-to-ceiling views of Lake Michigan. It had been the height of luxury, and a true measure of how far he'd come.

He looked around his current surroundings. A three-legged dog hopped across the lot a few feet away from him. The other vehicles weren't Bentleys or Audis or even Mercedes, but rusty pickup trucks and cars with mismatched hoods and plastic sheeting for windows. This wasn't a measure of how far he'd come. It was a measure of how far he'd fallen.

All he had ever wanted was to get off this rez. He could still remember seeing *The Cosby Show* on the working TV at a friend's house and discovering that other folks lived in great big houses where kids had their own rooms, water came out of the sink and lights turned on with the flip of a switch. The shock of realizing that some people had those things—and that those people weren't always white—had made him look at his childhood with brand-new eyes. The discarded trailer with cardboard patched over the windows and the holes in the roof? Not normal. Having to share a bed with his brother and mom? Not normal. Having to haul buckets of water from the stream and then hope he didn't get sick drinking it? Not normal. Not even acceptable.

Yeah, it sounded stupid to say that a sitcom had changed his life for the better. But at the age of eight, he'd realized there was a different life off the rez, and he wanted the big house, the fancy cars, the nice clothes. He wanted it all. And he'd spent his entire life earning it.

So being forced to come back to the rez felt worse than any demotion. If he hadn't been ordered to take this case—and if his future promotions didn't rest upon a clean victory—he wouldn't be here. Maybe he should have quit instead of taking this assignment. He didn't want to feel the stink of poverty on his skin again. It had taken years to clean the poor out of his pores. But he was the best at what he did, and what Nick did was lead lawsuits against energy companies. This was the kind of case he couldn't walk away from. This was the kind of case that made a person's career.

Nick shook his head, forcing himself to focus on what he was here to accomplish.

As the youngest junior partner in the history of the law firm of Sutcliffe, Watkins and Monroe, he'd won judgments for clients against BP for the oil spill in the Gulf, coal mines for the toxic runoff they dumped into the groundwater and even nuclear power plants with lax security. In the past five years, he'd gotten very good—and very rich—being environmentally friendly. He'd earned his place at the table.

Then his tribe, the Red Creek Lakota, had hired Sutcliffe, Watkins and Monroe to sue Midwest Energy Company for polluting the Dakota River when they used hydraulic fracturing, or fracking, to drill for natural gas. The tribe claimed the chemicals used in the drilling had seeped into the groundwater and contaminated the Dakota. They wanted Midwest Energy to clean up the water and pay for any health problems that resulted from the pollution. But this kind of case was beyond the scope of general counsel. The tribe's lawyer, Rosebud Armstrong, had needed someone who specialized in this kind of case. And that someone was Nick.

Nick had been surprised the tribe could afford the Sutcliffe, Watkins and Monroe price tag, but they'd recently built a dam and the funds from the sale of hydroelectricity had actually put the tribe in the black for the first time ever. *Of course* they'd picked Nick's firm. He supposed he shouldn't have been surprised that Rosebud had gone looking for him, but it still irked him. He'd always felt his tribe didn't want a damn thing to do with him when he was a dirt-poor nobody.

Now that he was a somebody who'd made something of himself, though, the tune had changed. No one had missed him when he'd left—not even Tanya Rattling

Blanket, his high school sweetheart. But now that they needed him and his uncanny ability to win in the courtroom, they wanted him to come home. Nick had been informed that the tribal council wanted him to lead the legal battle on-site. It wasn't enough that he had to work for people who'd rejected him. Now he had to go back and *live* with them.

Marcus Sutcliffe, the founder of the firm, had never been one to turn down a paying client. In no uncertain terms, Marcus had told Nick to pack his bags. And he did it in such a way that made it clear "no" was not an option. "Those are your people," Marcus had said, a look of distaste flitting across his face as he waved Nick away. "You handle them."

The hackles on Nick's neck still stood up just thinking about Marcus's dismissive tone. With a wave of his hand, Marcus had reduced Nick to the token Indian. His legal victories, top-notch law degree, his years of experience and dedication to the firm—meaningless, if Nick only earned them in the name of affirmative action. He'd fought for years to be recognized for what he could do, not what he'd been born. Apparently, he still had a long way to go.

The question Nick hadn't been able to answer was if Rissa Sutcliffe, Marcus's daughter, felt the same way. Nick didn't think so. He and Rissa had been dating for almost two years—exclusively dating for the last year. He knew she was attracted to what she called his "tall, dark and very mysterious" appearance, but that had never bothered him until Marcus had thrown "those people" onto the table.

But the fact was, if Nick won this case, he'd be first in line to succeed Marcus when he retired—an event that was only a few years off. So Nick nodded and smiled and acted like he was thrilled to be handling "those" people and their case. Better than giving the case to Jenkins, Nick's rival in the office.

So Nick wasn't here for the rez. He was here for his career. The sooner he won this case, the sooner he could get back to Chicago.

Then he took a deep breath, the smell of last night's rain and the grass surrounding him. No, this wasn't the Magnificent Mile. But that smell—the scent of wide-open spaces—was something he couldn't find in Chicago. Last night, he'd sat on his new front porch and done something he hadn't been able to do in two years. He'd watched the stars.

Maybe some time away from Sutcliffe, Watkins and Monroe would be a good thing. The interoffice sniping had reached new levels of Machiavellian backstabbing—so much so that Nick spent more time fending off sideway attacks from the likes of Jenkins than he did building cases. Some days, he felt less like a lawyer and more like a pawn struggling to be a knight.

If that had been all he'd been dealing with, Nick could have sucked it up and dealt with it. But it wasn't. For the last few months, Rissa had been buying bridal magazines and discussing an outdoor summer wedding versus a Christmas-themed wedding. Even Marcus had been calling him "son" more and more. On paper, that had been the plan—marry the boss's daughter and take over the family business. No doubt about it, Nick would have arrived. No one would have been able to take that success away from him.

Nick should have proposed to Rissa before he left to seal the deal. Should have, but didn't. He had always enjoyed Rissa's company, but he couldn't wrap his head around Rissa and the Red Creek Reservation in the same thought. Rissa wasn't exactly high-maintenance, but she required a certain amount of upkeep—shopping, spas, servants. Nick had enjoyed the hell out of being on the receiving end of that upkeep, but the moment the tribe had barged back into his life, his expensive lifestyle had suddenly felt forced. Almost unreal. Untrue, at the very least. Up until that exact moment, he'd been so certain of his plan, but now…he didn't know if he loved who Rissa was or the fact that she had been born a Sutcliffe. Which meant he was in real danger of being the world's biggest living hypocrite.

So he'd taken the job. He'd given Rissa a little talk about how some time apart would be good for them, help them know for sure if they were meant to be together. She'd taken it well enough, he supposed. "So you won't mind if Jenkins takes me to the Parade of Sails, then," she had said, her voice needle-sharp and her words just as pointed.

But Nick had already made up his mind. He was a big fan of clean breaks anyway. He'd reassured Rissa that she was free to see whoever she wanted, and when Nick's case was over, they'd "catch up" and "reevaluate" where their relationship stood. He needed a break from the whole lot of them—Jenkins, Rissa and Marcus. As much as he told himself he was back on the rez involuntarily, a small, hidden part of him was relieved to be here. Even though he was no longer the same man who'd left this rez behind, he still felt more like himself just being here.

The case would probably take a year, maybe two, before all the dust settled. That left him plenty of time to catch up with his family. He could look up Tanya Rattling Blanket for starters. True, he hadn't seen her in—man, it had to be almost two years—but he knew she was still here. She was one of those idealistic people who was determined to make a difference. She had made her preference for the rez over the real world clear back when they were dating. But if she was here and Nick was here, he didn't see any reason why they shouldn't be here *together.* As he remembered her, Tanya was whip-smart, bitingly funny and the kind of beautiful that most women spent their lives chasing and never catching. Thinking of Tanya was like watching the stars—he hadn't realized how much he'd missed her until he'd crossed the South Dakota state line.

In this distracted state, Nick walked into the tribal headquarters.

"Good morning, Mr. Longhair." At the sound of that voice, Nick tripped over his own foot and came to a stumbling halt. He looked up and saw Tanya sitting behind the front desk, wearing a fake smile and a pale pink blouse. "How are you today?"

For a moment, all Nick could do was stare. He hadn't seen her since the last time he'd come home to the rez, to celebrate his little brother's high school graduation. She'd been there, as radiant as he'd ever seen her. They'd done a little celebrating together—one more time, for old time's sake. Despite the fact that that had been almost two years ago, he suddenly felt as if it had been just last night. He remembered her as beautiful. He hadn't done her justice. His pulse began to pound. No, he'd been a fool not to realize how much he'd missed her—but now he did. "Tanya? What are you doing here?"

The fakeness of her smile grew more forced. "I'm the receptionist. Would you like some coffee?"

They'd dated all through high school, but their contact since then had been sporadic. Intense. Satisfying—

but only when he'd come back to the rez. He'd always been glad to see her, and this time was no different. Except this time, she didn't seem happy to see him. What—was she mad that he hadn't called? This wasn't the 1950s—she could have picked up the phone just as easily. But not calling was a small thing, and Tanya seemed one shade short of furious. They'd lost contact before. It shouldn't have been a big deal, but it felt huge. What were the odds that he'd wind up with coffee thrown in his face—or worse, his lap? Not in his favor. "No, thanks."

She stared at him for a few more seconds until he thought that smile was going to crack right off her face. "Ms. Armstrong is running late, and Councilwoman Mankiller is on a call. They asked me to show you around."

When he'd been here, Nick and Tanya had had the most intense, passionate relationship he'd ever been in. In the beginning, especially when they'd started having hot-and-heavy sex, he'd dreamed about taking her with him when he left. But Tanya wasn't the kind of girl who would blindly follow a boy to the ends of the earth. As much as he'd wanted her to go, she'd wanted him to stay. They'd had huge fights about it, then had the kind of makeup sex that made a man willing to admit that he'd been wrong.

In the end, the sex—and his feelings for her—hadn't been enough. He'd left. She'd stayed. Those were the choices they both had to live with.

Still, that wasn't enough to explain the animosity he was picking up on right now. The last time he'd seen her, she'd welcomed him back with open arms—and much more. The sex had been amazing—as passionate as anything he'd experienced with her before. He'd sort of been expecting the same kind of reception—but it was clear he wasn't going to get it. He hadn't exactly been burning up the phone lines during the years before he'd last been with her. She couldn't possibly have expected him to start calling just because they'd spent another night together—could she?

Nick squared his shoulders. He'd gotten very good at pretending he belonged someplace he wasn't truly welcome. Why should this be any different? "That would be fine, Ms. Rattling Blanket." He didn't need a tour—he'd been here before, in high school, when he'd come to talk to Rosebud about law school—but he wasn't about to stand in the lobby in total awkwardness until hell froze over.

She stood, her eyes cast down. She had on a slim gray skirt that hugged every inch of curves he didn't remember. She'd filled out—more generous breasts, a sweeter backside. Her hair was pulled away from her face, but it hung loose down her back. She looked *good,* in the primal sort of way that brought back memories of that last night together. What did those new curves look like? More important, what did they feel like? He had to physically restrain the urge to pull her into his arms. If he tried that right now, odds were good she'd deck him.

"This way." Without so much as a dirty look for him, she headed down the hall and opened a door on his right. "The conference room."

Why wasn't she glad to see him? As she stood with her back to the door, he leaned past her. His lawyer instincts told him to keep a safe, respectable distance from her, but he couldn't help himself. Her scent swirled around him—something soft and citrus and clean, all at once. Every second he was around her made him miss her that much more. All of a sudden, he found himself wondering how the hell he'd managed to survive the last two years without her smell, her voice, her face in his life. How had he survived without *her?* "I want to talk to you," he whispered in her ear.

A ruddy blush sprinted across her cheeks. Maybe he was imagining things, but he swore he felt the heat radiate off her skin. She'd missed him, too. He could tell by the way her pupils dilated and her breathing grew shallow. He knew that look. She'd been looking at him like that for as long as he could remember—usually right before she had begun ripping off his clothes. She could pretend to be all mad at him for leaving the rez behind, but he knew she couldn't deny the attraction that had bound them together since they were teenagers.

But she was going to try to deny it, that much was clear. She cleared her throat. "As you can see, the table and chairs are new." Then she shoved her shoulder into him, pushing him away. She shut the door and continued down the hallway. "This is Councilwoman Emily Mankiller's office."

This whole treat-Nick-like-a-clueless-outsider thing was starting to irk him, and the fact that she was fighting her obvious desire for him did nothing to improve his mood. "I know who Emily is. She hired me."

Tanya didn't even blink. She walked him past all the other council members' offices, ticking off familiar names, until they reached the end of the hall. "And this is your office." She swung the door open on a room so tiny that Nick was surprised to see someone had actually managed to wedge a desk into it.

What a hole. His coworkers in Chicago would be horrified. All of his desire ground to a painful halt as he was confronted with the professional embodiment of poverty on the rez. "This is a broom closet."

"Correction—it *was* a broom closet. Now it's the office of the legal counsel of the Red Creek Tribe." Tanya motioned to the desk, her hand brushing against the wall. "The computer is brand-new, and in theory, it prints to the copier behind my desk."

"In theory? I don't even have my own printer?" That was not good. Communal printing wasn't exactly the way to maintain confidentiality.

She glared at him, which was something of a relief. Better than being ignored. "You don't like it, you can leave. You're good at that."

He shut the door with more force than was required and turned to her. She tried to back away, but the wall didn't let her get very far. Her gaze darted toward the door. No way in hell he was letting her escape before he got some answers. He put his hands on either side of her shoulders, pinning her in. He wasn't touching her, but he could smell her. That was bad enough. "We both knew that night was a one-time-only thing. What's with you? I thought you'd be glad to see me." He cleared his throat. This close, he could see the way her pulse pounded in her throat. He could feel his own pulse matching hers, beat for beat. They'd always moved in harmony like that. That's what had always made being with Tanya so good. "I'm glad to see you. I missed you."

She flinched, but she didn't back down. "It's been two years, Nick. You clearly didn't miss me enough to visit. Not enough for one phone call."

"What was there to call about? You didn't want to come with me—you didn't want the kind of life I could have given you. And there's no way in hell I was going back to living in a shack on the rez. I thought it was best if we kept things neat and clean." Although "neat" and "clean" didn't exactly describe the effect she was having on him at this moment.

She glared at him, and he saw that the passionate feelings she had for him had changed somehow. Before he knew what was happening, Tanya had ducked out of his arms and was out of the tiny office. He faintly heard her say, "Red Creek Tribal Council, how may I help you?" and he realized way too late that he'd talked to her on the phone several times and never figured out that it was her.

Stunned, Nick sat in his new chair and tried to figure out what had just happened. He hadn't lied—he had missed her. Enough that seeing Tanya—and maybe rekindling their relationship—again had made the list of reasons to take the case and come home. She'd always understood him on a different level than any other woman had. That wasn't the sort of thing a man forgot.

But the woman answering the phone wasn't that same girl. Something had happened in the past two years. She didn't want to understand him any longer. She didn't even want to try.

The phone on his desk beeped, a loud, insistent noise that bounced around his new closet-sized office like a pinball. Nick jerked his head back. Man, that was going to take some getting used to. "Yes?"

"Ms. Armstrong is here, Mr. Longhair."

He had to give her this—she was a good receptionist. No trace of the argument she'd been winning lingered in her voice. "I'll be right out."

As he walked down the long hall, Nick got his head back in the game. Rosebud Armstrong was the general counsel for the tribe. She was here to get him up to speed on the current litigation status of the tribe. He was a lawyer, damn it. A good one. Youngest junior partner in Sutcliffe, Watkins and Monroe's history, and the only minority to achieve that accomplishment.

"How's Bear?" he heard Rosebud say. Curious, he slowed down. Did Tanya have a dog? Maybe she'd become one of those women who carried small dogs around in purses and put them in day care. Rissa had gone through a small-dog phase that still had Nick scratching his head. Some days, it felt like he'd never understand women—and this was shaping up to be one of those days. He wouldn't have figured the old Tanya for accessorizing with an animal, but then, he wasn't safe making any guesses about the new Tanya.

"Good. Mom spoils him rotten during the day, but…" Tanya's voice trailed off in a "what-can-you-do-about-it" kind of way. Sheesh, women and their dogs.

"I understand. How's the job going?"

The pause was longer this time. "Fine," Tanya finally said, and Nick could hear the forced smile from around the corner.

"I see." Rosebud's voice dropped from "lawyerly" down several notches to "coconspirator." "My earlier offer stands."

Offer? What offer? Nick didn't like the sound of that.

"You know I want to stay here. I've already learned so much. But…" her voice trailed off. "I'm going to see how it goes for now, but I might have to take you up on that."

He liked that even less. They were talking about him, weren't they? Finally, he wasn't able to take it anymore. He walked around the corner in what he hoped was a natural, non-eavesdropping kind of way. "Hello, Rosebud. It's good to see you again."

"Nick." She shook his hand and patted his arm, professional and friendly at the same time. He owed Rosebud a great deal. She was the one who'd pushed him to go to law school. More than anything in the world, he'd wanted off this rez. Rosebud had shown him the way to accomplish that. "How are you adjusting? Getting used to home again?"

He knew he shouldn't look at Tanya, but he did anyway. Just a quick glance, but more than enough for Rosebud to infer a variety of things. Tanya's attention was focused on her computer. "It's been a long time," was all he said.

Rosebud gave him the same look she'd been giving him since she'd written his recommendation letters for law school. That look combined a don't-screw-this-up scolding with a you-can-do-it sentiment. He hated that look. "A lot's happened since you left."

Wasn't that the freaking understatement of his life. "I saw you all built a huge dam."

Rosebud laughed in that polite way that said she was going to let him go this time. "You have *no* idea. Shall we?"

Tanya checked the clock—4:27 p.m. A whole minute had passed since the last time she'd looked. Would this day never end?

She wanted to get the hell out of here before Nick could corner her in the conference room or office again. At least, she needed to not get cornered. She'd be lying to herself if she said she hadn't felt the pull between them, or if she claimed she didn't want to feel it again.

She didn't know if that was because it had been two years since she'd last been with a man or what, but for a crazy second, she'd wanted him to kiss her. Which was strictly off-limits. She could not, under any circumstances, get involved with Nick Longhair again, not even for one night. Not after what happened that last time. And the time before that. After all the previous times, in fact. Only a fool would get involved with Nick Longhair and expect him not to leave her heartbroken. Tanya was no fool. Not anymore, anyway.

Besides, interoffice relationships were frowned upon. She needed this job. Councilwoman Emily Mankiller had hired her when Bear was two months old. Even though Tanya didn't think Ms. Mankiller would fire her without a good reason, Tanya felt like she had to keep proving herself. This job was the difference between having her own place and living with her mother.

What a mess. For twenty-two long, frustrating months, she'd dreamed of Nick Longhair walking back into her life like a white knight rescuing a damsel in distress. Tanya didn't know if she was a damsel, but being a single mother struggling to make ends meet provided lots of distress. Now Nick was back, and nothing about it felt like a rescue. Instead, it felt like a threat.

4:28 p.m. She wanted to get Bear, rush home and bolt the door. As much as she had dreamed about Nick coming back and sweeping her off her feet, now that he was here, he scared the hell out of her. What would he do when he found out about Bear?

If Nick found out about Bear, he could want nothing to do with him—or her. He could accuse her of getting pregnant on purpose, like she'd been trying to trap him. He could flatly deny he was Bear's father. He could cut her out of his life permanently. In some ways, he'd already done that. This time, though, there would be no hope for her to cling to, no bright, shiny fantasy of Nick coming back to her. It would just be the end.

That thought was terrible enough, but Tanya knew it wasn't the only possible outcome. Nick could decide he'd always wanted to be a father. He'd always talked about kids, back when they were wild-eyed dreamers without two nickels to rub together. Now Nick had all the nickels he had ever wanted. Did he still want kids? Maybe he did, maybe he'd outgrown that dream—just like he'd outgrown Tanya. Tanya knew any fatherly interaction would be on Nick's terms, and his terms alone. He had already decided that Tanya wasn't good enough for him—why else would he have bailed on her without a second look? What if he decided that she wasn't a good-enough mother? If Nick wanted to, he could take her son—their son—away from her. He could run her into the ground in a courtroom and take Bear to Chicago. She'd be lucky if she got to see him once a year. She wanted to think Nick wouldn't do that to her, but she didn't know the man he'd become. She wouldn't put anything past him.

"So that about wraps it up for today." Rosebud and Nick walked into the lobby, heads down, feet dragging. "When should I plan on coming back in?"

"Give me a week to get up to speed," Nick said, cranking his neck from one side to the other, "and then I'll give you a call."

"Done." Rosebud stopped and looked at Tanya. Tanya's heart began to pound. Of course Rosebud had figured out that Nick was Bear's father—she was the smartest woman on the rez. But most people hadn't connected those dots. Tanya preferred it that way. Rosebud's gaze slid back to Nick. "You should come out to dinner some night. My husband has an interesting perspective on fracking. Tanya knows where we live."

Great. Any less subtle, and Rosebud would be beating Nick over the head with a sledgehammer. "Maybe we'll do that," Nick said. "If Tanya's up for it."

Up for being alone in a car with Nick for the drive out to Rosebud's house? Hell, at this exact moment in time, Tanya wasn't sure she was even up for breathing. Besides, she didn't even know what "fracking" was. Yes, she'd learned a lot in ten months, but that was general stuff about tribal operations. She wasn't allowed in on closed-door meetings yet. She was still just the receptionist, but she was working on being the best darned receptionist she could be. It beat the hell out of frying burgers at a fast-food joint an hour off the rez while fighting morning sickness, which was the job she'd held when she'd found out she was pregnant.

"You can let me know," Rosebud said, letting it drop. "But think about it."

Rosebud headed out, leaving Nick and Tanya alone in the lobby. For a few moments, neither of them moved. Nick looked out the front doors; Tanya stared at her desk. His head was held high, his shoulders back. Everything about his stance said that he was in control of this—or any other—situation. She'd always loved his ability to take control of any situation, but now it scared her. For her part, she was afraid to do anything but work on that breathing thing. What would Nick do now?

He pivoted on the balls of his feet. "Ms. Rattling Blanket, I'd like a word with you in my office."

Her heart sank. He knew about Bear, and he was going to demand his rights. Wouldn't it be wonderful if those rights took the form of Nick realizing what he'd left behind and deciding that, finally, he would stay? But given how fast Nick had hightailed it out of town the last time, she wasn't going to get her hopes up. He may have come home, but for how long? He'd made his point crystal clear. He was too good for the rez. He was too good for her.

Determined to maintain a level of professionalism, she grabbed a pen and a legal pad. When she made it to his office, the door was open and he was sitting behind his desk. That was a good sign—he wasn't going to try to trap her again. Not right away at least. "Yes?"

"Sit down." He didn't look up from the document he was reading.

Tanya did as she was told. She felt a little like a lamb going willingly to slaughter.

Nick kept reading his paper. Why, oh, why did he have to look so good? It wasn't fair, she decided. Why couldn't he have gained forty pounds of beer gut or lost his hair while he was gone? Maybe grown a few warts—anything that would make it easier for Tanya to not miss him.

But no. He seemed taller now, and any weight he'd gained appeared to be pure muscle. His shoulders were broader underneath his crisp white shirt, his sleeves neatly cuffed at the wrists. She'd noticed his pants earlier. They looked expensive—nothing like the frayed jeans he'd always worn before. The light from his computer caught on a huge silver watch around his wrist. He wore those new, expensive clothes like he was born in them.

But the worst of it was that he'd cut his hair. He'd sworn he'd never do that. He was a Longhair. It went with the name. Instead of reaching almost as far down his back as hers did, his thick black hair was closer to his ears and slicked back.

He glanced up and caught her staring. "What?"

"You cut your hair." Lord, that's not what she'd wanted to say, but the words just popped out. She'd meant to keep their interactions strictly professional.

One side of his mouth curved up in a smile. Was

he flattered that she'd noticed, or was the new-and-improved Nick just vain? "Occupational hazard," he explained as he ran a hand through his close-cropped mane. "Where do you live now?"

She could not believe the audacity of this man. He'd all but fallen off the face of the planet for almost two years without sparing a single thought to her, but the moment he arrived back on the rez, he expected to pick up where they'd left off? No. Not gonna happen. She had her pride. And a mountain of bills. But she'd rather cut off her own foot than let Nick think she needed his money. She'd already made a mistake with him once. No way she was going to make it again.

So she didn't answer. Several seconds passed before Nick realized that she wasn't talking. "Tanya? Did you hear me?"

"I'm sorry." Strictly professional. No need to get fired for insubordination. Not yet anyway.

A shadow crossed Nick's eyes. She had his full attention now, and she was pretty sure that wasn't a good thing. "Do you still live with your mother?"

"I'm not sure what this has to do with my job." Or yours, she wanted to add, but that whole insubordination thing kept her mouth shut—for once.

His eyes narrowed. Combined with the expensive clothes and the new hair, Tanya realized she was sitting across from a complete stranger. "You're not going to answer my question?"

"Is there something else you need help with? If not, I have to go. Councilwoman Mankiller lets me leave at 4:30." She'd never needed to get Bear more than she did right now. But no matter what Nick did next, she could claim to have acted with all due respect.

Moving slowly, Nick set the paper aside. He put his

hands facedown on the desk and then leaned toward her. Tension rippled between them. She could just catch a whiff of his cologne—something that smelled exotic and expensive. Even though she knew she was in danger of being trapped, she couldn't pull away. Nick did that to her—drew her in and never gave her the chance to get out. All it had ever taken was for him to give her that half smile as he moved in on her, just like he'd tried to do in the conference room earlier. He must expect that she'd come running at his beck and call, just like she always had. The problem was, when he cornered her earlier, she had still wanted to come running. Just thinking about how close he'd been made her ache with a desire that she'd thought she'd long since buried. She took another deep breath, pulling his scent in deeper. She wasn't sure if she even wanted out, not with the way his eyes flashed at her. He was like the mountain lion, using his silky brown eyes to hypnotize his prey—her—before he moved in for the kill. Then he said, "I'm going to find out one way or another. I'd feel better if you told me."

There it was—the very real threat Nick Longhair posed to her life and to her child. One way or the other, he'd get what he wanted. The only difference was whether she got in his way or out of it.

Without rushing, Tanya stood. He might have all the power in this room, but she was going to be damned if she let him take her dignity. "Have a nice evening, Mr. Longhair."

Someone should have a nice evening. But it wasn't going to be her.

Two

Nick didn't show up at Tanya's little house that night. At work the next day, he walked in at 9:00 a.m. like he owned the place, gave her a heated stare and headed back to his office. He was still in there when she left at 4:30 p.m. He never even asked her for coffee.

She spent another restless night shooting out of bed at the slightest noise to make sure Nick wasn't prowling around outside. She doubted that he was the sort of fellow who prowled anymore, but once upon a time, before he'd left her the first time to go to college, he'd made a regular habit of tapping on her window at three in the morning and taking her on a joyride in whatever truck he'd "borrowed" across the otherwise-silent rez.

Those middle-of-the-night trips to nowhere had been when they'd talked about their dreams and nightmares. "When I leave this rez, I'm not gonna be a dirt-poor Indian anymore, Tanya. I'm gonna be rich. I'm gonna be *somebody,*" he'd muse, laying on a blanket, the night air cooling them off after the heated sex. "I'm gonna buy you diamonds and pearls and the biggest house in South Dakota. And our kids—they're not gonna live like this. Our kids are gonna have the best of everything. Rooms full of toys, new clothes that fit, their own ponies—everything." The way he'd always said it made it clear that was all the stuff he'd wanted and never got.

She'd loved him for wanting to take care of her. But Tanya had always told him the same thing. "I don't need all that stuff, Nick, not as long as I've got you."

At the time, it had all seemed like a bunch of wild talk. She hadn't realized how serious he was. But then, she hadn't realized how serious *she* was.

Tanya had left the rez once, too. She'd gone to college at the University of South Dakota in Vermillion, just about two hours from the rez. She'd gotten her B.A. in Native studies with a minor in political science. When she'd first left home, she'd finally understood what Nick had always talked about. Everyone there had a car and an apartment, it seemed, with nice clothes and computers and stereos. The jealousy had been crushing.

That had changed the day she'd walked into her first political science class. She'd signed up because Nick had already been accepted to law school and she'd assumed that knowing more about politics would be a good way to support his career. But instead, the professor—some leftover relic from the 1960s counterculture—had gone on and on about how a single person could take on the political establishment and change things for the better.

Yeah, that guy had fried half his brain on acid trips back in the day, but that didn't mean his words carried any less weight with Tanya. It had been then that she'd realized she could make life on the rez better—if she didn't abandon it. She had to stay and change it from the inside. A fact made all the clearer by her time working as a fry cook. Minimum wage at a dead-end job didn't help her tribe. It didn't do her any favors either.

So she'd gotten Councilwoman Emily Mankiller to mentor her and had taken the receptionist job at tribal headquarters after Bear was born so she could have a front-row seat for the local political show. Things had changed now that the tribe had money. Tanya knew that Nick was here for a lawsuit against Midwest Energy, but everything was done behind closed doors or in low whispers. It was clear that Tanya wouldn't be able to be a part of that conversation—not while she was a receptionist anyway. Some days that irritated her, but the posturing and maneuvering wasn't her strength. Tanya was more concerned with making sure people had enough to eat and heat in the winter. No back-room plotting needed. Even though she was just the receptionist, she could say she was already making a difference. She kept a running tab on who was about to have their power shut off, who's health was failing too fast and which kids needed another hot meal. Those were small things, but they counted. Sure, she could make a bigger difference if she had an ally who was good at the behind-closed-doors stuff. In fact, Tanya had always hoped that Nick would bring his fancy law degree back to her and the rez. Together, they could change things for the better. Together, they'd be unstoppable.

But Nick hadn't come back. Until now.

Another noise outside had Tanya up again. 3:15 a.m. Tomorrow was going to be a long day, but at least it was Friday. She looked out the window, half hoping to see the old, carefree Nick out there. That was the Nick she'd loved since the day she'd turned twelve. She could still remember the jolt of electricity that had coursed through her when he'd ridden up to her birthday party bareback on his paint pony—and shirtless. He'd just turned sixteen—so out of her league—but that hadn't stopped him from sliding off the horse right in front of her, leveling that devastating smile at her and handing her a hand-picked bunch of wildflowers with a "Happy birthday, Tanya," thrown in for good measure. It had seemed like he was her present, already half-unwrapped. Tanya had fallen and fallen hard. Nothing and no one could ever compare to Nick.

Sure, he had hardly looked at her for a few more years, but by the time she'd turned fourteen, he'd given her her first kiss. By the time she was fifteen, she'd given him everything.

Part of her wanted that life again—where the only cares she had in this world were how she could slip out without waking up her mom to steal a few more hours with Nick. But there was no going back, and there was nothing outside but a full moon. Nick had come back only twice in the past six years—when he graduated from law school and for his brother's high school graduation. She'd asked him to stay that first time, while the scent of their sex still hung in the air. "Stay with me," she'd said, and even now she cringed at how pathetic the words had sounded.

"Babe, I have a life now," had been his reply. He'd said it gently, like he knew he was tearing her heart out with a single swipe. True, he'd told her she could stay with him if she came to Chicago, but it was the kind of halfhearted offer that begged not to be taken up.

No, he had a life now. A life that didn't include her or their homeland.

She got back into bed and checked on Bear. He was

curled into the little baby ball that had his bottom sticking up into the air.

Tanya smiled. She didn't need Nick's money or diamonds or houses. She didn't need any of that stuff, as long as she had her son. She was tied to this land by blood—the blood of her ancestors and the blood of her son. She couldn't abandon this place because that would be the same as abandoning part of her soul.

She couldn't leave.

Not even for Nick Longhair.

By the time she got home the next night with Bear in tow, Tanya was beat. Nights like this made her wish that she could afford a television and pizza delivered to her door, because Bear was being clingy and her head hurt and the three hours until Bear's bedtime seemed like a month.

The whole week, all Nick had done was walk in, give her "the look" and disappear into his office. He didn't ask for coffee, tell her to make copies or demand to talk to her. Despite her resolution not to fall under his spell again, she still found herself daydreaming about him at least trying to sweep her off her feet. He'd corner her in the conference room, shut the door and press her against the wall. If she closed her eyes, she could actually feel the length of his body against hers—the way they fit together as effortlessly as they always had. He'd kiss her until she couldn't breathe. Of course she'd rebuff his advances—in her fantasy, she could just walk away from him.

Reality was different. Would it kill him to at least notice her? She couldn't even be in the same room with him—for however short a time—without being painfully aware of him. As much as she tried to hate him—and heavens knew she tried—she couldn't shake the hope that somehow, some way, they'd go back to the way things had been. Despite having a child now, a big part of Tanya still felt like the same girl she'd always been—the girl who loved Nick.

But no. Maybe she'd just guessed wrong about him. This new-improved Nick wasn't the slightest bit interested in the same-old Tanya. Why would he be? She wasn't model-perfect, rich or anything else like the women he'd probably spent all his free time with back in the big city.

Maybe this was just how it was going to be, she thought as she boiled the water for the mac 'n' cheese. They'd just keep pretending like they'd never been in love. She'd keep Bear's existence quiet. They'd be like *sicas,* spirits, passing through each other's lives. It could work.

This way of thinking lasted until she put Bear down at eight. She read him a story, sang him his bedtime song and rubbed his back until his little eyelids closed. Finally, she thought as she shut the door behind her and sagged against it. Exhausted as she was, she needed at least a half hour of peace and quiet before she went to bed. She trudged down the short hallway that separated the bedroom/bathroom half of the house from the kitchen/living room half, turned the corner and let out a scream.

There, sitting on her couch, was Nick Longhair. His tie and jacket were gone and his shirtsleeves were cuffed, but otherwise, he looked exactly like he had when she'd last seen him this morning. Next to him sat a robin's egg–blue gift bag.

A jumble of thoughts ran through her head. She was positive she'd locked the door. He looked horribly out of place on her ratty couch. Had he noticed the laundry basket of toys on the other side of the room? Damn it, why did he have to look so good? What was in the bag? She felt like hell and probably looked worse. Which all came out as, "What are you doing here?"

He sat there, giving her that same damned look for what felt like an hour. Did he think she would throw herself at him? If so, he had another think coming. "You look good, Tanya."

Part of her all but vibrated with the compliment. For a delusional second, she wasn't a schlumpy mom with mac 'n' cheese in her hair, but the crazy-in-love girl Nick had wanted. Oh, how she had missed the way he made her feel. She'd missed being that girl.

The other part of her didn't like where this was going. If he thought he could just waltz into her house and expect her to fall into his arms only to see him waltz right back out of her life for another two years, he could go to hell. She'd even buy him a handbasket. "What do you want, Nick?"

"I brought you a present," Nick said, sounding completely unconcerned with her rudeness. He stood and handed the bag to her.

She didn't want to look. Well, she did, but she was afraid that it would be something weird or stupid and that would further grind her fantasy about Nick's return into the dust. She was also terrified it might be something really nice, but she wasn't sure why. "It's nice to see you didn't forget about the tradition of bringing gifts."

"I didn't forget about a lot of things."

The way he said it—all serious and intent while he looked as if he'd spent two years wandering in the desert and she was a tall, cool glass of water—sent another spike of heat through her body.

She should not let his good looks and generous gifts and intense gazes get to her. He'd not only ignored her for two years, but he'd also ignored her the entire week. She needed to stay strong and make sure she protected herself and her son from the kind of heartbreak that Nick seemed to specialize in. Nick would leave again, as sure as the sun rose and set, and Tanya would have to pick up the pieces. It was bad enough picking up her own pieces. She didn't want to have Bear shattered, too.

She would not be seduced. Now she just had to keep telling herself that. "Gosh, you could have fooled me. Why are you really here, Nick?"

A shadow flashed over his face, but it was gone as quick as it had come. "I picked it out for you."

Her hands were shaking, which was irritating. Why was she so nervous about this? In the space of a second, she found herself wishing she was taller, thinner, smarter and more reserved. But she wasn't. Except for the extra baby weight, she was exactly the same girl she'd always been. And that girl hadn't been enough for Nick.

She opened the bag. Inside was a huge bag of Skittles and a pink elephant with a big, blue bow around its neck.

Tanya's throat closed up as her eyes began to water. She tried blinking, but the tears kept forming.

"It was our first real date, remember?" She was startled to hear Nick's voice so close to her ear. She was even more startled to feel his hands slip around her waist. He'd sneaked up behind her, damn it, and now he was hugging her. That simple touch was enough to break her. His scent surrounded her. She couldn't escape it. She couldn't escape her past with Nick, so she didn't even try. "Our first real date, because I was able to get a truck. I took you to that county fair and bought you Skittles because they were your favorite and won you a pink elephant shooting that water gun."

As he spoke, he pulled her back against his chest until the heat from his body was searing the flesh on her back and underneath his hands. No, she hadn't been imagining that he'd added muscle—she could feel the hard planes of his body crushing against her.

Nick pressed his mouth against her ear. "Remember? How we took the long way home and got lost and pulled over on that dirt road?" His lips brushed over her lobe, sending a shiver through her that she couldn't have stopped if she'd tried. "Remember how bright the stars were? Remember how beautiful you were? I didn't forget our first time, Tanya. Tell me you didn't either."

"No." That one word was all she was capable of saying. A bag of Skittles and a pink elephant were just enough to bring that night rushing back to her. She remembered being scared and excited and so in love with him.

The more things changed, the more they stayed the same. A decade had passed since that night, and there wasn't anything she wouldn't give to go get lost down that dirt road with him again.

A *whump* came from the bedroom. Oh, no. Oh, *hell*. That was the sound of Bear flopping out of bed. As far as Tanya could tell, Nick didn't know about the boy. It was up to her to keep it that way.

"What was that?" Nick asked, pulling away from her.

"Nothing." Tanya spun and threw her arms around his neck, holding him in place. "Let me thank you for the present." Then, against her every better idea, she kissed him.

It wasn't supposed to be the kind of kiss that took

all of her resolve and smashed it to bits. She was just trying to distract him from the sound of Bear jiggling the doorknob. But it didn't work that way. Nick folded her back into his arms and just like that, the distance between them was gone and all Tanya could think was that Nick had come back for *her*. When he held her tighter, heat rushed down her back and pooled lower.

Oh, she needed him, in a primeval, instinctive way that had nothing to do with reason or logic and everything to do with the thrill of Nick's tongue sweeping into her mouth. God, how she'd missed this feeling of being wanted and needed—of being loved. No one had ever loved her like Nick had, and she knew no one ever would. Was it wrong to want this? Was it really wrong to want him?

As the kiss deepened, she almost forgot why she'd kissed him in the first place. Twenty-two long, sexless months pushed her deeper and deeper into his arms until she shook. But then another thump cut through the desire—the sound of Bear banging his tiny fist against the door because he couldn't work the knob. Nick jerked his head away. "Is there someone else here?" He let go of her and headed toward the bedroom door.

"No—no one else." Tanya threw herself in Nick's path. "Just me." She plastered what she hoped was a sexy smile on her face in an attempt to hide her panic. "I, uh, wish I had a truck. We could go for another ride somewhere." Anywhere Bear wasn't.

Nick's eyes zeroed in on her as Bear took up a steady pounding rhythm. He took another step forward, forcing Tanya to take another step back. "You're not alone? Are you living with someone?"

The way he said it, like she'd been cheating on some poor, imaginary guy by kissing Nick, was enough to remind Tanya of all the reasons why she shouldn't fall back in love with Nick under any circumstances, ever again. He wasn't here because he loved her or trusted her. He was here because she was convenient. "No."

Bear was now banging on the door with both fists. Tanya could tell because by now, Nick had her pinned against the door. "You're lying to me."

"What, that noise? It's, uh, nothing." She scrambled to think of something believable. "A dog. I have a dog. With a big tail. Knocks into stuff all the time. What can you do?" She tried to laugh as she put her hands on Nick's shoulders. "He, uh, jumps. And sheds. We should leave him alone. Don't want him to mess up your nice pants after all."

She tried to push him back, and he let her. Then, at the last second, he pivoted, letting her momentum carry her right past him. He caught her arm to keep her from falling over at the same time he turned the knob and pulled open the bedroom door.

Bear stood there, silent tears running a race down his fat cheeks. He took one look at the strange man who held on to his mommy, opened his mouth to scream and didn't make a sound.

He never did.

Tanya's heart sank. The jig was up. It was time to face the music. "Dang it, Nick, you scared him." Tanya jerked out of Nick's grasp and scooped up her little boy. "Hush, sweetie." Which was a pointless thing to say, but she said it anyway.

She held Bear and rubbed his back until he stopped flinging his arms around. His head rested on her shoulder and she could tell he was sucking his thumb. She wasn't sure if he'd gone back to sleep or not until he reached up and laced his chubby fingers into the end of her braid. He was awake. Scooting around Nick, she went to the fridge and got him a sippy cup of water.

While Bear drank, Tanya watched Nick, who was staring at the boy. His mouth hung open as his eyes took it all in. One thing was clear—he hadn't known she'd had a baby. He didn't know she'd had *his* baby.

Maybe she could still keep it that way?

That was just the desperation talking. Now that Nick knew, he wouldn't rest until he knew everything. How long would it be before he took Bear away from her? How long would it be until he left her all alone again?

While this irrational fear—at least, fear she hoped was irrational—clogged up her throat, she struggled to keep her face calm and blank. Do not panic, she tried to tell herself. Don't give it away. "Well?" Because he was going to say something, sooner or later. And she didn't think she could wait on later anymore. She just wanted to get this over with.

"You have a baby?" Nick's voice wobbled.

Tanya felt a small thrill of victory that she'd managed to outsmart the smartest man in the tribe—for a little while anyway. "Yes."

Nick shook his head, like he couldn't trust his eyes. "He's not mine, is he?"

The question was a punch to the gut. She couldn't have imagined a lower insult coming out of his mouth. She'd loved Nick Longhair with every bit of her heart and soul since she was in sixth grade and he'd been a freshman in high school. She'd done everything he'd ever asked of her—even going into debt to go to college so he wouldn't be ashamed of her. She'd planned on spending the rest of her life with him. Never once had she strayed—and this was how he repaid her devotion. By leaving her all alone and then assuming she'd been stepping out on him.

The whole deep-breathing thing wasn't working so good. "He's mine. That's all you need to know."

That came out louder than she meant it to, because Bear jerked and started thrashing. Nick fell back a step, like he was afraid of the baby. Men, she thought with a snort.

Nick regained his composure. "What's wrong with him?"

"Did you come here just to insult my honor and mock my son? Because if that's the only reason you're here, you can just take your expensive clothes and your short hair anywhere else but here." Bear jerked in her arms and began rolling his head against her shoulder. He didn't like it when she yelled.

Nick looked at her for a nerve-racking second before he stood. Then he was closing the distance between them. He stopped just short of touching her or Bear. "That's not why I'm here."

"Then why are you? Why did you come back?" God, he was driving her mad. He'd always driven her past the point of rational. Why would she have expected that to change?

"Hi, guy. I'm Nick." He reached over and took one of Bear's small hands in his. "It's nice to meet you."

Bear looked at this strange man for a moment longer before he buried his face back in Tanya's neck.

"What's his name?"

"Edward, but everyone calls him Bear."

"Bear." He nodded in approval as he placed his hand on the top of Bear's head and patted. "That's a good, strong name. It's nice to meet you, Bear."

Tanya refused to be pleased that he liked it. She was

done pleasing Nick. But she didn't know what to say next that wouldn't come out as an accusation or, worse, an insult, so she kept her mouth shut.

A look of peace came over Nick's face, erasing the hard, lawyerly edge. In that instant, he was the man Tanya had loved with her whole being. He had come back to her—to them. She wanted to love him again. In that instant, she did.

It didn't last. The peace disappeared and the edges came back, sharper than ever. Nick's gentle pat suddenly seemed like he was holding on to Bear—with no intent of letting go. "Tell me, Tanya, how old is he?"

Nick would leave again. He would *always* leave. But she knew that this time, he wouldn't go alone.

He would take her son.

Three

Nick leaned against the doorway to the bedroom, his gaze fastened on Tanya. God help him, she was a born mother. The way she held that little boy while she sang him an old song about mockingbirds pulled at Nick's heart in a way that was strange and discomforting. Her voice hung on to each note in the song, filling the room with her quiet power. Somehow, she was even sexier now than before. Maybe it was just those curves, but that wasn't enough to explain the almost-magnetic attraction he had felt this whole week. That was why he'd kept his distance at work. And with good reason. Right now, he was having trouble keeping his hands off her.

Nick counted backward for the twentieth time that night. He'd come home for his brother Jared's high school graduation two years ago. No, he remembered—not exactly two years. Twenty-two months. Tanya had been at the party. It had been the first time he'd seen her for almost two years, but she'd been irresistible. He'd assumed she'd moved on while he'd been away, but she'd only had eyes for him.

They'd left the party separately, but he couldn't get her off his mind. Just like the old days, he'd tapped on her window in the middle of the night. That night had been some of the most intense sex he'd ever had, before or after. No one compared to Tanya. It was just that simple.

That night had been twenty-two months ago.

How old was that baby? Based on his size, Bear couldn't be much more than eight or nine months old. Not that Nick was an expert in children, but even he knew that smaller meant younger and bigger meant older.

However, that basic fact didn't mesh well with the fact that the child had gotten out of bed, tried to open a door and settled for banging on it. Again, he was no expert, but Nick was pretty sure that babies didn't start walking or opening doors until they were a year old, give or take. Nine months of pregnancy plus a thirteen-month-old baby would put Nick firmly into the potential-father category. Nine months of pregnancy plus an eight-month-old baby would rule him out.

How had the fact that Tanya had a baby gotten past him? Even as he asked himself that question, Nick knew the answer.

He didn't talk to people on the rez anymore. Now that he thought about it, he hadn't talked to anyone but his mother, and she only called every few months to demand money. Being made the youngest junior partner in the history of Sutcliffe, Watkins and Monroe, one of the most prestigious law firms in Chicago, failed to impress Mom. His perfect record in the courtroom was

meaningless to her. She could care less that he was the
first minority to achieve that accomplishment. All she
cared about was how much money he had, and how
much she could get him to send her.

Now that he thought about it, Nick did remember
getting a couple of messages from Tanya. At the time,
he'd assumed she was just having a hard time letting go
and moving on. He'd justified not returning her calls as
a clean break—for both of them.

Of course, if the break had been that clean, would he
be standing here in her little house now? He doubted it.

Had she been calling to tell him about the baby? Or
had his mother been telling everyone how he was rolling
in dough, and Tanya had merely decided to get her cut?

If the boy was his, then Tanya wouldn't have let a
few misplaced messages keep her from telling him. She
would have called and kept calling. She wouldn't have
left him out—that wasn't the girl he'd known.

But then, neither was the Tanya who was out for
money. She'd never cared about wealth—she'd told him
so hundreds of times, back when they were dirt-poor
Indians dreaming big. And if she was after the money,
wouldn't she have thrown that baby in his face the moment he'd set foot back on this rez, demanding child
support? She hadn't. She hadn't said a word. Nothing
about her actions reminded him of the girl he used to
know.

But then, the woman in front of him wasn't that
girl either. Beyond the appearance of luscious, womanly curves—curves that took every noble intention
of his and blew it to hell and back—Tanya didn't look
at him with the same adoration—the same, well, *devotion*. More than anything, she seemed pissed that he
was here.

Nick looked around the tiny house. As houses on the rez went, it was quite nice. The windows were intact, the electricity was hooked up and the plumbing featured running water. The house was a hell of a lot nicer than the trailer he'd grown up in. By that lousy standard, she was doing well for herself. She didn't need his money. Not desperately anyway.

But compared to the penthouse apartment he'd left behind in Chicago, this place was a dump. No other way to describe it. The house was smaller than his bathroom had been, with just an open kitchen/living room combo—he couldn't use the term "great" room because it was anything but great—and a single bedroom. With no crib.

He flicked a piece of peeling paint off the doorframe and hoped to hell it wasn't lead paint. Tanya wasn't his. Maybe the kid wasn't his. But he'd cared for her once, and it hurt to see her living in a hellhole like this. Grinding poverty made him defensive.

Tanya turned a slow circle as she rocked that baby to sleep. Her dark eyes flicked over him with brutal efficiency, as if he didn't live up to her standards. Nick had had enough of that crap in law school. The only standards he lived up to were his own.

Tanya continued to turn until the face of that boy—Bear, Nick corrected himself—was in view. His little eyes were at half-mast, with one thumb in his mouth and the other hand buried in the end of Tanya's braid. He was cute, as far as babies went. His round face looked so much like Tanya's, but Nick couldn't see any of himself in the boy.

Something was wrong with that kid. Wasn't hard to see that, or to notice Tanya's hyperdefensiveness. The boy hadn't whimpered, much less screamed, since Nick had opened that door. Sure, he'd opened his mouth, but no single noise had escaped his body. The only sound had been his banging on the door. That wasn't natural, Nick knew, and it bothered him. If Bear was going to grow up to be a Lakota man, he had to have a voice. A man needed to be able to make himself heard.

He'd always liked the concept of kids. In the back of his mind, he'd always planned on having a few—three, at least—and having the perfect family life. For a long time, he'd envisioned Tanya beside him at the Thanksgiving table or snuggled up to him as the kids opened present after present on Christmas morning. Just like the Cosbys, only Lakota. True, his life in Chicago had put those plans so far on the back burner that they almost fell off, and he was sure Tanya wasn't open to the idea. The problem was, none of the women he'd dated in Chicago were the least bit interested in having a big family. But he kept telling himself that as soon as he made partner, he'd slow down and settle in.

Nick knew that he would be a good father—the kind of man who went to his kid's T-ball games and helped with science fair projects. All the stuff he'd missed out on as a kid. Nick's own father had been long gone for years. True, Nick had turned out okay—thanks to Bill Cosby—but his little brother Jared hadn't. Mom said he was getting clean in prison. Jared wasn't the only member of the tribe who'd gone down that path. Nick knew it would break Tanya's heart if the same thing happened to Bear. The boy needed a father.

Assuming, of course, Nick was the father. And if he wasn't, where was the guy? Why wasn't he here helping out? What kind of jerk knocked up a sweet, smart girl like Tanya Rattling Blanket and then left her high and dry?

The tightness that hit him midchest was as hard as any punch. Love at first sight, part of his brain noted, categorizing this new feeling and comparing it against all previous emotions. He'd never fallen in love at first sight. Lust, sure. He was a man after all. But this was different. He had no idea if Bear was his son or not— probably not—but all the same, he knew he loved the little guy.

Tanya eased off the bed and gave her son one last look before she turned to where Nick was standing. However, she didn't meet his gaze as she tried to slide past him.

Nick wasn't having any of that. He took hold of her arm and leaned down to whisper, "What's wrong with him?" in her ear. The smell of her—now he could tell it was soft baby powder underneath lemons—hit him in the nose and collided with that tight-chest feeling until he was dizzy.

She jerked her head back enough to glare at him, but he saw past the pissed and noted how her lower lip had the slightest of trembles. He wanted nothing more than to kiss that lip until the rest of her was trembling in his arms, but he didn't. That wasn't why he'd come here. Although he was having a little trouble remembering his original motives at this exact moment in time.

Tanya looked back at the bed for a fleeting second before she jerked her chin toward the other room. Nick nodded in agreement and followed her out into the living room. He didn't let go of her arm, though. He just slid his hand down until he had a hold of hers. That basic touch was somehow reassuring. Or maybe the reassuring part was that she didn't shake him off like a fly.

He expected her to stop in the living room, maybe sit on the ratty sofa. He expected her to pour her heart out to him, maybe lay on the sob story and then hit him up for some money. He'd seen that enough in Chicago.

But she didn't. Instead, she pulled him right outside, underneath the fading crimson of a late-summer sunset. The moment had all the markers of being special—beautiful woman, perfect scenery, a reunion—but before he could do anything remotely close to kissing her, she spun on him, pulling her hand free. "Why are you here? You had a job in Chicago. You made a lot of money. Your mom said so. You weren't a dirt-poor Indian anymore."

The brutal truth of those words—his words—smacked him upside the head. He'd said that out loud. To her. "I did okay."

"That's what you wanted, wasn't it? Why did you come back?" She didn't shout it, but the forcefulness of her voice would have made the most cynical lawyer sit up and take notice, and Nick wasn't that cynical yet.

"The tribe hired my firm."

"But why you?" Her insistence was not comforting.

"This case is my specialty. And no," he added quickly, cutting the words off before they could leave her mouth, "I can't tell you anything about it if you don't already know." Truthfully, he hadn't had a choice. It had been either take the case or find a new firm, but that sort of admission wouldn't get him anywhere. As Nick knew all too well, perception was often more important in negotiations than reality. Time to redirect this conversation. "I wanted to see you again, Tanya." He couldn't help himself. He leaned in closer, catching her scent on his tongue again. It was insanity to want to taste all of her, but he did.

"I called, Nick. I left messages. But you never called me back." Her voice lost all of its fierceness, and her eyes dropped to the ground. When he took that last step and closed the remaining distance between them, she put her hands on his chest. Clinging to that distance, he thought as he circled his arms around her waist. He should take the hint and back up, but he couldn't. He had to feel her in his arms right now. "You were just gone."

Part of him wanted to yell at her. She might never admit it, but Nick knew what she had really thought all those years ago—that he'd fail out there in the "big city" and come running back to her. Well, he hadn't failed, and he sure as hell wasn't running back to her. He hadn't returned her calls because he hadn't wanted her to think he was pining for her. He had tried to tell himself that he didn't need her—he didn't need anyone. He could take care of himself. Couldn't she see that?

Except here they were. The moment he'd been able to get away from his case, he'd come right to her, expecting to find her waiting for him. No, not expecting—*wanting*. He wanted her to be waiting for him, for her to be happy to see him. She hadn't been happy to see him at the office, but he'd told himself that was the professional thing to do, to keep their relationship quiet. Instead, she'd been trying to keep that baby quiet. She hadn't been waiting for him at all. It was almost as if she hadn't even missed him. He'd been working a hundred hours a week to prove to her that she should have had more faith in him, that she should have come with him, and now he didn't even know if she'd given him half a thought in all that time. The sudden realization that perhaps he needed Tanya more than he was willing to admit left him feeling vulnerable. He didn't like feeling vulnerable. It left him in a dangerous position of weakness.

He couldn't let her see that weakness. He couldn't

let her know that she meant more to him than he did to her. The problem was, he couldn't fabricate excuses to pacify her valid arguments either. She had him dead-to-rights. He could spout off excuses about being busy or being involved, but those were nothing more than excuses, and she was smart enough to see right through them. His only option was to go at her sideways. Maybe, just maybe, if he could get past her defenses, he could show her how much he really needed her. Then maybe they could go back to what they'd been before. He touched his forehead to hers and used his height to push her head back. "But I'm here now." His lips grazed her temple, then her cheek. "God, I missed you, Tanya."

She stiffened, and then pulled away. Suddenly, Nick was standing alone halfway between her house and his car while she was on her front stoop. She crossed her arms and glared at him. "Did you, now."

He'd envisioned this going a little better. Smoother. More sensuality, less defensiveness. This conversation needed to move in a different direction. "I got a house in Sioux Falls. It's only an hour away." Mom had asked if he wanted his bed back, but there was no way in hell that Nick was going back there. It wasn't the same hovel he'd grown up in—he'd sent Mom money to get a better place—but emotionally it was still a hellhole. "It's got a gourmet kitchen and a huge master suite." It also had two other bedrooms and a fenced-in backyard. A nice family home, the Realtor had said. But he wasn't about to make it sound like he wanted Tanya to move in with him because that hadn't been the reason Nick had taken it. The real reason was that it was the nicest place on the market in southern South Dakota, and even then it cost less than a quarter of what the condo in Chicago was worth.

"You *bought* a house?" The way she said it made it sound like he'd blown all his money on a gold-plated umbrella stand or something equally frivolous, not invested in real estate, and certainly not like she was angling for an invite.

"I'm just renting."

The moment the words left his mouth, he knew he'd screwed up. The kind of open-mouth-insert-foot blunder that sunk careers in seconds.

Tanya's face fell, and then fell some more before it disappeared under a blank, almost soulless mask. Any relationship they had had, or were going to have, was sinking, the decks blazing under the weight of his honest fireball. There would be no chance of raising this ship.

His stupidity made him desperate. "Tanya, wait—how old is Bear?"

"What does it matter, Nick? You're renting. You won't stay." She turned and took a step into her house, but before she shut the door, she looked over her shoulder. Maybe it was a trick of the setting sun, but he thought he saw a tear race down her cheek. "You never do."

Four

Monday came whether Tanya wanted it to or not. Part of her had come to terms with the fact that Nick knew about Bear. She'd never been that good at keeping secrets anyway. He would have found out sooner or later. Sooner had been the winner, that was all.

The other part of her was a wreck. Nick finding out about the boy hadn't erased her worries, only replaced them with a different, larger set. What would Nick do next? He couldn't be happy with her. Odds were decent he was furious with her. She might have guessed what the old Nick would have done, but this new man? No idea. She'd be lucky if he didn't sue her into oblivion, most likely.

She didn't have to wait long to get an answer to that particular question. Nick walked in at his regular nine o'clock and gave her the same look he'd given her all last week. Just seeing him again made her heart beat faster. But this time, he added, "Ms. Rattling Blanket, I'd like to see you in my office."

Damn it. At least he wasn't going to keep her on pins and needles the whole day. She grabbed a notepad and a pen and began the long walk back to his broom closet. The whole time, her stomach did flips. She knew he could grind her into the dust if he wanted to. He was too good a lawyer and had more money than she ever would. Tanya didn't want to go down without a fight, but she was outclassed and outgunned, and she knew it. She kept telling herself that she had to protect Bear from Nick's abandonment, but she knew deep inside that she had to protect herself.

She wished she hadn't kissed him, no matter how wonderful that kiss had been. By letting him past that first physical barrier, she'd reminded herself in Technicolor of how Nick had always made her feel, of how he could still make her feel. The danger was, she still wanted that feeling. One stupid kiss was more than enough to show her that she still wanted Nick.

Nick was seated behind his desk. She was glad to sit in the chair because her knees didn't feel like they were up to the task of holding her upright. "Yes?"

Nick didn't look up. Instead, he kept reading a huge file and taking notes in the margins. "What's wrong with Bear?" There wasn't a trace of tenderness in his voice.

Dread started flipping around in her belly with the nerves. Tanya knew what this was. "You'll find out one way or another, but you'll feel better if I told you, right?"

Nick's pen stopped moving, but he still didn't look at her. Tanya preferred it that way—not seeing his eyes made it easier to remember that she didn't know this man. "That is correct."

She sat there, willing her knees to stop knocking. Nick turned a page, almost as if he'd forgotten she was there. A flash of anger made Tanya furious. She was sick and tired of being forgotten by Nick Longhair. By God, she would make sure he'd never forget her again.

"The doctor says there's a problem with his ears. He gets a lot of ear infections, and he might be completely deaf. There's something wrong with his vocal cords, too." She paused, realizing how bad this must all sound. But she had Nick's attention now. He'd set his pen down and was watching her. "That's why he sleeps in the bed with me. I was nursing him, and he doesn't cry. He just sort of...shakes. I was afraid I'd sleep through it when he really needed me." Good Lord, that sounded even worse. What kind of mother couldn't get her kid medical care? What kind of mother didn't even have a separate bed for her baby? The kind that couldn't take care of her child. The kind that shouldn't have custody. "I'm not a bad mother," she hurried to add, feeling stupid that she'd just given Nick all sorts of ammunition to use against her—if he wanted to.

Did he want to?

Nick shut his eyes, looking disgusted. With her. "How old is he?"

This was it—the ultimate way to make sure that Nick would always remember her. "He was only five pounds, seven ounces when he was born, but he was two weeks late." She swallowed, trying to maintain a level of professionalism when the situation was anything but. Nick was a smart guy. She was willing to bet he could do the simple math of pregnancy and age in his head. "He'll be one next week."

The air in the small office chilled, as if frost was settling around them. Nick rubbed the bridge of his nose,
then ran his hands through his still-too-short hair. He
looked upset. Of course, if anyone made "upset" look
good, it was Nick. Even now, he wore his angst hand-
somely.

Well, he could just be upset. Tanya held her ground.
In a way, it was a relief to have the weight of the secret
off her shoulders. But she was just too terrified of what
Nick would do next to enjoy it.

Of course, he didn't do any of the worst-case scenar-
ios that Tanya had envisioned. Instead of blowing up,
accusing her of child neglect or threatening her with a
lengthy custody battle, Nick pushed his reading mate-
rial aside and pulled out a leather-bound journal and
a gold pen. Of course he had a gold pen. He probably
had gold toothbrushes and a gold towel bar, just to impress his rich lawyer buddies. "Besides a crib, what else
does Bear need?"

He sounded tired, but not as upset as he had looked
moments before. That was the most unusual thing of
all. At least Tanya had been correct in assuming she
had no idea what Nick would do next. It was nice to be
right about something. "He doesn't really—"

Nick cut her off with a wave of his hand. "Yes, he
does. He's a year old now, and I'm sure that if he needs
to wake you up, he'll throw something at you."

Tanya took a deep breath. She didn't want to lose her
temper. Just because he wasn't upset now didn't mean
he wouldn't come after her later, and Nick could use an
outburst to paint her as a violent woman in court. "As I
was saying, he doesn't really need a crib. He'll be able
to crawl out of that soon. A toddler bed would be better."

Now Nick did look up at her, half a smile on his face

making him look devastatingly handsome. This would be so much easier if he wasn't the man of her dreams—physically, at least. She wished she could find him disgusting or repulsive, but no. He had to be some sort of demigod over there. Tanya refused to buckle to his good looks. She would not get hysterical, furious—or turned on. "Good point. What else does he need? I want to get him some things for his birthday."

"We're fine, really." What Bear really needed was the kind of stuff that one didn't wrap up in bright, shiny paper with a bow—quality day care, fresh fruits and vegetables, medical care. None of those things made for a fun birthday party.

"I'll get him a car seat for my car," Nick said, pointedly ignoring her. Tanya saw that her plan to make sure Nick never forgot her again had instantly failed. He had no interest in her. His only concern was the boy. That realization made the dread in her stomach churn at an even faster rate. "He's beyond one of those walker things…maybe there's a baby store in Sioux Falls? I'll check that out this weekend."

"You don't have to do that." More to the point, she didn't want him to do that. Was he trying to buy her off? She didn't want to be in his debt. Owing Nick would be almost the same thing as being owned by Nick. She didn't want to become another thing he owned.

"Yes, I do. He's my son, isn't he?" It wasn't a question, not really. She realized he was trying to get her to say the words out loud. She refused to give him the satisfaction. Nick let his not-question hang for a few moments before he went on, "It's my responsibility to take care of him."

Tanya cringed at the implied criticism. What, did he not like the job she'd been doing? Of course not. Nothing in her world was ever good enough for Nick Long-hair. "You're a little late to this party. He's almost one."

"Because you didn't tell me. I'm not a psychic, you know."

He was going to blame this on her? Fat chance. The surge of anger pushed aside the dread. It felt good. Anger was power. She might not have the money or the connections, but she still had a hell of a lot to say, and he better believe he was going to hear it. "What was I supposed to do, Nick? I called. I left messages with a snooty-sounding secretary. You never called me back. Was I just supposed to show up? Plop a baby into your lap in court? Would they have even let me in the door?"

He opened his mouth, but she cut him off. She wasn't about to give him the chance to charm his way out of this. "No, they wouldn't have. And you know why? Do you remember the last thing you said to me? 'Been good seeing you, Tanya. Have a nice life, Tanya.' And then you drove off without a look back, like I didn't mean anything to you."

That was what had hurt the most. The fact that Nick had finished, zipped up and walked away without even so much as a how-do-you-do. That had hurt her worse than everything else combined. A lump tried to catch in her throat, but she swallowed, forcing it back down. No way in hell she was going to cry in front of Nick. "What part of that said, 'Call me if you get knocked up'? What part of that said, 'Call me' at all? I'm not dumb. I know when I'm not wanted."

"I didn't say that." The words were out fast—too fast. It was nothing more than a knee-jerk denial. "In fact, if I recall correctly, I asked you to come with me. You're the one who said no. You're the one who talked about our ancestors and our land. I've got news for you—this isn't my land or my ancestors' land. It never was. This is the worst land in the entire country—the bone the government threw to our ancestors because no one else wanted it. Why, on God's green earth, you want to stay here and fight for this place is beyond me, Tanya. It always was."

He was seriously going to make this whole thing her fault? "Get your facts straight, Nick—or is that no longer a requirement of the legal profession?" He snorted, but she wasn't done with him yet. "You did ask me to come with you, but that didn't happen two years ago. That was when you graduated from law school—or did you forget that, too? You didn't ask me to marry you. Instead, you went on and on about the great place you were going to get and the cool car you were going to drive and all the things you were going to buy. You didn't talk about us. Just about stuff. You made it sound like you were looking for someone to split the rent with. Why would you think I'd abandon even the worst piece of land in the country to be your roommate? You're the one who thought you deserved the very best, Nick. Did it ever occur to you that I deserved the best, too? And that sure as hell wasn't the kiss-off you gave me last time."

"I was *trying* to give you a better life. It's not my fault you didn't believe I could really give you one. You'd already turned me down once—what was I supposed to do, keep asking so you could keep kicking me down?"

Wait, what? But before Tanya could process what he'd just said, he stormed on. "And I'll have you know that under no circumstances did I tell you to have a nice life," he repeated. His voice was firm, bordering on dangerous, but Tanya saw the doubt in his eyes. This wasn't the knee-jerk denial—this was damage control.

He didn't remember. He could talk a good game about never forgetting his first love and all that crap that was custom-built to make her think she was important to him, but she knew the truth. He had forgotten about her. She tried to say words to that effect, but that stupid lump kept moving up, so instead she just glared at him.

Still, it was nice to see that Nick was still capable of emotion. Right now, for instance, he looked guilty. Really, *really* guilty. That made her feel better. "You mean something to me, Tanya," he offered up weakly. "You always have."

Her anger bailed on her, and instead she was gripped by an overwhelming sadness. She couldn't even glare at him. "But I don't mean *enough,* Nick. Not as much as the big city and the big job and the big house means. Not as much as you mean to me." Just saying the words out loud made that unavoidable truth hurt even more.

"Tanya, I'm—" His apology was cut off by the distant ringing of her phone.

Which was just as well. She didn't want to hear his forced, halfhearted apologies. She scooped up her notebook and pen and walked out of his office with her head held high.

She loved him desperately. She always had, and she always would. But she would never ever be able to hold him. And that, more than the accidental pregnancy, more than life as a struggling single mother, was one of the great tragedies of her life.

Luckily, she was used to living with disappointment.

Tanya supposed she should have been surprised to hear a knock on her door two nights later, but by this point, she was fresh out of astonishment. She knew it was Nick by the way he knocked—three firm, hard raps that made it clear he wouldn't take "no" for an answer.

Great. It wasn't enough that Nick's presence pervaded her working hours. No, he had to barge in on her family time, too.

He's part of the family, a nagging little voice whispered in the back of her mind, but Tanya shut down that kind of thinking fast. He was the provider of a set of chromosomes, that's all.

Before she opened the door, she took a deep breath and reminded herself that she was not to fall for anything Nick said or did. If he was here, he would probably try to sweet-talk her again, like he had the other night. But if he thought he was going to get a second kiss, he had another think coming. "Yes?"

Then she sucked in even more air. Nick the lawyer wasn't on her front stoop. Instead of the button-up shirt and dress slacks, he was wearing a faded pair of blue jeans and a T-shirt that wasn't skintight but was close enough to make her heart flutter. His hair wasn't as slicked down either, but looked more tousled, like he'd been driving around with the top down.

Nick, part of her brain sighed in swoon-worthy fashion. The Nick she remembered. The only thing that was missing was the horse. Sure, those jeans had probably been made to look that broken in—for a heck of a lot of money, no doubt—but they rode low on his hips. She wanted him to turn around so she could see how they fit the rest of him.

"Hiya, Tanya." The way he said it—low but in his old accent and with just a touch of teasing—made it clear that he knew what effect he had on her. She half expected him to ask her to go for a ride with him. It didn't matter that she wanted to say yes, because that would be a mistake.

Even just standing here with a good three feet between them, Tanya could feel the pull of Nick's body. All the fires she'd accidentally stoked with that ill-advised kiss last week began to heat her from the inside out.

Already, her mind was attempting to rationalize her undeniable attraction to Nick. Would one more time really be such a bad thing—as long as they used protection? Surely, two mature, careful people could take care of certain…needs together without things getting messy again. As long as she didn't fall back into that hopeless, pining kind of love again, surely she could get a little physical relief. Scratch a Nick-sized itch, such as it was. And who better to help her out than the man who already knew what she wanted and knew how to give it to her? The very object of her fantasies? No awkward getting-to-know-you phase, no more ugly surprises. Just two consenting adults doing a little scratching. It didn't have to be a big deal.

She shook herself. The last time she'd strained with this level of absurd justifications, she'd wound up with Bear. She couldn't make that kind of stupid mistake again.

Nick was still standing there. She realized she had no idea how long she'd been lost in her own little world. Apparently long enough to make this awkward, because Nick said, "Is it okay if I come in?"

Tanya realized his arms were filled with bags bursting at the seams. "What is all that?"

He waited until he was inside before dropping all the stuff with a *whump*. "I got some stuff for the baby—I mean, Bear."

From where he'd been throwing his Cheerios onto the floor from his high chair, Bear's head snapped up. He wriggled so hard that Tanya had to get him out and set him down before he tipped the whole thing over. In his herky-jerky baby way, he walked over to where Nick was pulling board books and balls and big, chunky cars with flashing lights out of Super Mart bags. "Do you like cars?" he asked Bear, who clapped his hands with excitement. "Here," Nick said, handing the boy a fire truck. "Try that one on for size, big guy."

While Bear chewed on the ladder, Nick kept unpacking. The next bag held a bunch of clothes with the tags still dangling off the sleeves. Pants, shirts, shorts, T-shirts with cartoon characters on them—more clothes than Bear and Tanya had put together.

"I didn't know what size he needed, but I figure that kids grow, right?" Nick didn't wait for an answer as he started unpacking another bag. This one was full of more winter clothes, including a huge coat. "So I got some twelve to eighteen months, some eighteen to twenty-four months. You can take them back if they don't fit."

Tanya was stunned. How much money did he spend on all of this? A couple hundred at least. To him, it was probably just another day, but all of this stuff was more than she could afford in a year of careful scrimping and saving. How sad was it that she was even considering returning some of it just to get the cash? She could get enough to take Bear to a doctor, maybe even enough to pay for the prescription this time.

Nick took a pair of winter boots and a cute stuffed bear out of the last bag. "Here you go, Bear. Your very own bear."

Bear grabbed at the animal. Tanya felt her head shak-

ing. Nick had come prepared, and Bear was too young
to know he was being bought off.

"This is too much," she started to say, but Nick cut
her off.

"The toddler bed is back-ordered, so it'll be two
weeks." He ducked his head and shot her a sheepish
smile. "I couldn't figure out the car seat, though. Might
need a little help with that."

"We can't accept this." She didn't have much, but
she had her pride. And she wouldn't let Nick put a price
on it.

Nick's eyes hardened—not much, but enough to let
her know that he didn't think too much of her opinion.
"'We'? Or just you?" He looked down to where Bear
was now chewing on his new bear's nose. "I think he's
happy to have some nice things."

"Because the only things I can give him are complete and total crap, right?" Tanya struggled to keep her
voice calm, but she didn't do a good enough job. Bear
looked up at her with worried eyes.

"I didn't say that."

"Admit it—you don't think I'm a good mother."

"I didn't *say* that." Nick had the same controlled,
pissed tone to his voice. "Stop putting words into my
mouth."

"Where else should I put them? I have a few sug-
gestions."

She expected Nick to come back at her with both bar-
rels blazing, but instead, he smiled—and then laughed.
Bear watched them for another moment before he broke
out in a toothy grin and went back to chewing on his toy.

"What?" she demanded, feeling foolish and not
knowing why.

He closed the distance between them in two long

steps, and before Tanya could stop him or react at all, he'd wrapped his arms around her and placed a fire-hot kiss on her forehead. "I know you won't believe this, but I *have* missed you, Tanya. No one in Chicago talks to me like you do."

Tanya's arms shook with the effort not to return the favor and pull Nick's hard chest closer to hers. She wasn't being swayed by any compliment, any tender gesture. None of this was working. Really.

He leaned down, his voice quiet and only inches from her ear. The warmth of his breath rolled down her skin until a lot more than her arms shook. "I'm going to be here for at least a year. You don't have to love me, babe, but let me see my son. A boy should know his father."

That was a damnably low blow, one that blew past her anger and went straight for her heartstrings. Who would she be hurting if she fought to keep Bear from Nick? Sure, she could exact some revenge for Nick's repeated abandonment of her. But in the long run, it was Bear who would suffer. Would she really do that to her son?

Could she really do that to Nick?

As if he could feel that the attention of the adults had shifted away from him, Bear launched the teddy and began to flail. Tanya took a step toward him, but Nick put a hand on her shoulder. "I got him," he said, a peaceful smile on his face.

Tanya watched as the man of her dreams swooped her son up into a big hug and then grabbed a board book and settled down to read him a story about a very hungry caterpillar. Tears swam across her vision.

She couldn't keep Bear from Nick. She just couldn't.

But what would letting Nick back into her life do to her?

Five

Throughout the evening, Nick could feel Tanya watching him. She stared while he read Bear stories. She kept an eagle eye on him as he and Bear rolled a ball back and forth on the floor. And she hovered behind him as Nick fumbled his way through his first diaper change. She didn't tell him he was doing it wrong, though. Hell, she didn't say anything. She just watched.

Nick didn't remember all the words to the bedtime song Tanya had sung the other night, so he stuck with the classic "Twinkle, Twinkle, Little Star." Of course, while he sang it, Tanya stood in the doorway of the small bedroom, a look on her face that drifted between irritated and hopeful, with a dash of worried thrown in for good measure.

In other words, she looked confused.

That bothered Nick. What about this situation wasn't black and white? He was Bear's father, and as such, he had certain rights and obligations. He had a right to spend time with his son, and a correlating obligation to provide financial assistance for his care. Now that Nick was aware of the situation, he planned to step up to the plate and be a father.

So the situation with his son couldn't be what was worrying Tanya, which only left one other possibility. She was worried about *him*.

And that bothered him, and the fact that it bothered him was a problem in and of itself. When the hell had he gotten to be such a nice guy? He had the legal upper hand here, and they both knew it. Tanya had admitted Bear had health problems and that she couldn't afford proper medical treatment. Gaining custody would be a walk in the park. If he were still in Chicago, he'd use those facts to maximize his advantage. That was how the game was played. The moment someone showed weakness, whether it was opposing council or a co-worker, you had to use that weakness to your advantage.

Tanya's passions ran deep and true, and up until now, he had never viewed that as a weakness. He'd never viewed her as weak at all. Headstrong, stubborn, passionate—yes. Especially the passionate part. Nick knew he tended to be overly analytical. That trait made him a damn good lawyer, but he'd been accused of being cold and, on more than one occasion, heartless. Tanya's passion had always been the perfect counterpoint, whether they were arguing about tribal politics or having incredible sex.

Of course, the flip side of the game he played in Chicago was that anything you said and did could be used against you, too. What would Marcus Sutcliffe think if he knew Nick had fathered a disabled bastard? More than likely, he'd scoff in an unsurprised way and say something like, "What do you expect from one of *those* Indians?"

Even thinking about Bear like that made Nick feel sick to his stomach. How could he define his own son that way? He knew the answer—that's how it would look in court. But that would be the same as dismissing Nick as the token Indian. No way was he going to let people slap a label on his son, because the moment they did that, Bear would spend the rest of his life trying to live that label down.

Nick looked down at the boy, his thumb in his mouth, his eyes half-closed. That tightness hit his chest again. He would do whatever it took to make sure that Bear wasn't dismissed. He needed a voice, and Nick was in the position to give him one.

Did Tanya understand anything about the games Nick was used to playing? She couldn't, because she'd never shown up in Chicago with the baby. A person with less-than-sterling morals would have made dangerous threats of exposure in hope of extracting some money. Extortion was the legal term, but it would be blackmail, pure and simple. Nick saw it happen all the time.

But Tanya wasn't like all those other people. It was apparent that she had no idea how much power she held in this situation. And even if she did, he didn't think she'd use it. Somehow, despite her dirt-poor upbringing and barely-getting-by lifestyle, she had managed to remain pure and uncompromised. Hell, she'd even tried to refuse his gifts, despite how much she obviously needed them. Nick couldn't remember the last time he'd dealt with a person who wouldn't play the game. While it was refreshing to know that she couldn't be bought, it left Nick with the unsettled feeling of knowing the rules had changed but not knowing what they'd changed to.

Nick's morals were just shy of sterling. Maybe he'd played the Chicago games long enough that he'd been permanently tarnished. Winning primary custody of Bear would be easy—he could steamroll Tanya in a courtroom without breaking a sweat. He could get his son out of this hellhole of a rez and take him to Chicago. He could give Bear the finest medical care, the best schools, the nicest things—all the advantages that Nick had only dreamed about as a kid. He didn't need Tanya's permission. He could do whatever he wanted. Part of him wanted to do just that—show her exactly what he'd accomplished without her. She hadn't let him give her a better life—that was her problem. But Nick didn't have to let her withhold that life from Bear. In fact, he could make a strong argument that it was his moral imperative to gain primary custody of his son. He had worked his butt off for the last four years, amassing a small fortune and an unstoppable reputation. The least he could do was to share the benefits of all his hard work with his son. Then, maybe Tanya would finally realize that he hadn't been selfishly focused on himself, but working for a life they could live together.

But he didn't want to steamroll her. He didn't want to be the one who took everything she held most dear and ground it into the dirt. Maybe it was being back under the wide South Dakota sky, or maybe it was the little boy who was almost asleep in his arms, but Nick didn't want to win at all costs this time. Oh, he still wanted to win, but he didn't want to salt the earth behind him. Tanya had always meant something to him. He didn't want to destroy that. He didn't want to destroy *her*.

He tried to set Bear down just like Tanya had done the other night, but got his arms crossed up and wound up flopping the kid onto the bed. He froze, terrified he had just woken the baby up again, but after an extra-deep sigh, the little guy rolled over. Nick looked to Tanya, hoping to see approval or a smile on her face, but was surprised to see that she'd already turned away. In fact, if he didn't know any better, he'd say she was sprinting down the small hallway.

Moving as quietly as he could, Nick followed. By the time he got the bedroom door shut, she was out the front door. Oh, no. No way she was going to run away from him now.

At the very least, they had to work out a visitation schedule, and he had to know more about Bear's health—especially if he was going to start paying the medical bills. Tanya was still healthy, and Nick had never had any issues. It couldn't be normal for Bear to have so many massive health issues. There had to be an external cause. Maybe it was just because Nick had litigated so many major pollution cases, but his first thought was that that external cause was environmental. What were the odds that Bear's silence was connected to the contamination of the groundwater that the tribe maintained had occurred as a result of Midwest Energy's fracking?

But if that was the case, why wasn't Tanya just as sick? That was the part that didn't make sense to Nick, so he had no justifications for jumping to conclusions. He wasn't going to rule anything out yet. All this meant was that he needed to do a little more research. The boy was going to have to get tested. If there was a chance he could be cured or fixed or whatever, Nick had to make sure that happened. And if the results happened to bolster his case, well, he'd have another piece of evidence in his pocket.

But environmental concerns were not the real reason

he took off after Tanya. Despite it all—her rejection of him, the hidden baby with health problems, the adversarial tone to their interactions—he wanted her. While he was fully aware that she'd kissed him out of self-defense the other night, there was no way she'd faked the heat that had flowed between them. He could still taste her desire on his lips. All that was complicated and tense had disappeared in that hot moment until he'd forgotten about lawsuits and reservations and everything that wasn't Tanya. He needed Tanya. It wasn't any more complicated than that.

Except it was. It always had been. Maybe it always would be, because by the time he caught up to her, she was standing next to his Jaguar, arms crossed and an unassailable look on her face.

Right. As much as he wanted to feel her body in his arms again, if he forced the issue, he would do more harm than good. He couldn't let her know that he needed her more than she needed him. Never ever show weakness. "Like I said, I was having a little trouble with the car seat."

"Have you considered that the problem wasn't the seat, but your car?" She spoke stiffly, but he could still hear a tiny tease in her voice.

He was glad to hear that tease, however small. "Are you suggesting that a two-seater convertible is not the ideal family car?"

"We aren't a family," she snapped, then took a step forward and wrenched the passenger door open.

Nick sighed. She wasn't going to make this easy on him, but he supposed he had that coming. "I read the instructions," he offered. "I couldn't find the LATCH things it said to use."

She hauled the car seat from where he'd wedged it

in the passenger seat and set it on the ground. "Because car seats don't go in the front." She gave his Jaguar another once-over. Most women—in fact, all women—swooned over his car. Proof positive that Tanya wasn't like anyone else, he figured. "But I see you are sadly lacking in a backseat, so…"

Then she flipped the car seat around and shoved it back into the car. After several unproductive pushes, she turned around, and, hands on hips, gave him a stern look. Her hair had come loose from her braid and floated around her face, and her cheeks were pink from the effort. Heaven help him, she was beautiful. He hadn't guessed she could be more attractive than he remembered her, but those curves, that fire in her eyes—he had a few more less-than-sterling thoughts.

"You push from this side," she said, slipping around the back of the car before he could do anything rash like kiss her.

Before he understood what she was doing, Tanya had climbed in through the driver's-side door and was hauling on the car seat. Then he heard it—the sickening sound of plastic scraping against his custom burl-walnut dash. "Stop!"

She paused. "It's the only way to get it in." The way she said it made it clear that she thought he was choosing the car over the kid.

He wanted to tell her that it was a very expensive car, but he knew that observation wouldn't go over real well. Instead he leaned over the seat, making sure to brace it so she couldn't keep scraping up his woodwork. "He shouldn't be riding in the front seat anyway." Clearly, he was going to have to rethink this plan. "Maybe you could bring him out to my place this weekend?"

Tanya's eyes bored into him. He realized that his

face was less than a foot from hers. "This may come as a surprise to you, but I have plans."

Her tone kept rubbing him the wrong way. Yes, he had earned a little flack, but that didn't give her the right to treat him like the enemy. She was just as much a culpable party in this as he was. She'd stayed here of her own choice, so she could quit treating him like he'd abandoned her. As far as he could tell, he was not the bad guy here, and the sooner she stopped treating him like he was, the easier things would be. "This may come as a surprise to *you,* but not everything I say is a direct attack on you."

She held his gaze without flinching. He leveled his most effective glare at her, and she met him head-on. Despite the attitude, he was impressed that she didn't buckle. "So you're leaving indirect attacks on the table."

He was about to cut her down to size—he did *not* need all this resistance in his life—but then the corner of her mouth curved up and the angry lines faded from around her eyes. And just like that, she was radiant.

The air between them seemed to thin, making it hard to breathe. Relinquishing his grip on the car seat, he reached up and smoothed an escaped strand of hair away from her face before he cupped her cheek in his hand. "I *have* missed you, Tanya."

She leaned into his touch, her eyelids fluttering—but not quite closing. Instead, she opened them wide. The confrontation was gone; instead, he saw desire just below the surface. This time, it wasn't hiding behind ulterior motives. It was right out where he could see it.

"I don't have to love you." She tried to throw his words back at him, but she couldn't stop the way her voice shook. He could feel that tremor through his hand.

It was a small thing, but he still felt it throughout his entire body.

Mentally, he pumped his fist in victory. For once, she didn't have a barb ready to throw at him. "But you still *care* for me, don't you?" *You still want me* is what he really wanted to ask, but that would be pushing too far, too fast. Besides, Tanya was smart enough to know what he'd really been asking.

She dropped her gaze, her face flushing with a different sort of heat. Nick could hear the *yes* on her breath. He could see it in her eyes. But she didn't say it. Instead, she pulled away and backed out of the car.

He'd lost her. Maybe she was better at playing this game than he thought. But he wouldn't let his disappointment show. Part of playing the game was not letting the other side know when they had you on the ropes. He stood. Tanya stood by the driver's door. He could feel the weight of her expectations. He just wasn't sure what she expected of him. She wanted him, that much was clear. But she didn't trust him. Though she seemed open to letting him spend more time with Bear. Maybe he'd been wrong earlier—this situation wasn't as black-and-white as he wanted it to be. Not for her anyway. "I'd still like to see Bear this weekend." Of course, he'd like to see Tanya, too, and preferably without a car between them.

"You're welcome to come with us."

Was he mistaken, or was there a challenge in her eyes? "Sure, I could do that. Where are you going?"

No, he wasn't mistaken. She was throwing down the gauntlet. "There's a powwow in Platte." Her smile grew menacing. "I'm sure everyone would love to see you again."

Nick's mouth ran dry. He'd been to powwows before. He'd done his fair share of dancing. But that had been a long time ago. A lifetime ago, some would say.

Powwows were big deals on the rez. Everyone came for the food and the dancing. Which meant everyone would be there. All those people who he hadn't seen in years—people who still lived in crappy trailers, who still drank themselves into a stupor. His family would be there.

Everything he'd tried to escape.

Tanya was waiting on an answer. Nick knew he should say something smooth, something that wouldn't knock her opinion of him down another notch—"Sounds great" would be a good start—but he couldn't do it. It was bad enough to work in a hole of a broom closet, worse to see his son living in near-poverty. He couldn't bring himself to willingly lower himself any more. He was not going to be one of "those Indians," damn it. Not for Tanya. Not even for Bear. Not for anyone.

And to think, just a half hour ago, Nick had been sure Tanya didn't play any games. Well, she'd played him—right into a corner. And the only way out was through her.

So he went on the offensive. He couldn't help it. She had him trapped, so he had to do an end-run. "How many of those people know I'm Bear's father? No one at the office seems to have a clue."

It worked. "What?"

"My own mother never mentioned you had a kid. Did you tell people you had a one-night stand after a weekend of drinking? Immaculate conception? Who did you name as the father?"

If he were half the lawyer he thought he was, he wouldn't be letting the crestfallen look on her face make him feel the slightest bit guilty. She'd backed him into a corner—he'd just returned the favor. He should not feel bad for her.

But he did, damn it all. Her eyes watered, but he had to admire her self-control, which kept those tears from spilling over. "He was small," she said, the fierceness in her voice at odds with the wounded expression on her face. "People assumed he was premature. No one suspects *you*." She spat the last word out like she'd expected to eat some chocolate and gotten a Brussels sprout instead. "And I don't expect you to come to the powwow. I wouldn't want you to debase yourself. God forbid you act like an Indian, Nick. God forbid you *be* an Indian."

He watched her storm back into her dinky house and slam the door. At least he'd been right about one thing. No one in Chicago talked to him like Tanya did.

He wasn't sure if that was a good thing or not.

Six

Tanya walked around the outside of the dance circle. Well, walked was a strong word. She lurched around it, with Bear holding on to both of her hands as he smiled at everyone and every thing—even a bear headdress got a grin. The elders sitting in lawn chairs patted Bear on the head; a few dancers in full regalia swooped him up and spun him around. The red, black and yellow fringe on Bear's dance shirt whipped around him, almost as if the yarn was laughing out loud for him.

She loved coming to the powwows. When she'd been younger, she'd competed in the fancy shawl dance, her fringe spinning as much as Bear's did this afternoon. However, now that she was older, she preferred to do the traditional dance. The fringe still swayed, but not with the same fervor.

Tanya chatted with people as they made the rounds. Socializing was a huge part of the powwow, but she also took mental notes on who needed to have a hot meal delivered or who was in danger of having their power shut off this winter. One of the reasons she stuck with the receptionist job at the Tribal Council was that Councilwoman Mankiller would sit down with her once a month and listen to Tanya's "news from the front," as she called it. If there was enough money in the budget, Councilwoman Mankiller authorized Tanya to pay an electric bill or do the grocery shopping for the elders. It wasn't a lot, but Tanya could say she was making life better for her tribe, one meal at a time. That was why she'd wanted to be on the Council in the first place— once she had some real power, she'd be able to move up from one meal, one bill at a time to wider initiatives. She'd love to get a real grocery store opened on the rez—that would bring in some local jobs and provide better food choices than what was available at the Qwik-E Mart gas station. But she had to build up considerable political capital to do that. That was why she hadn't taken Rosebud Armstrong up on her offer to be the legal secretary for her private practice. Tanya had to pay her dues, and she wanted to stay on the front lines where she could make a difference now.

Of course, her position as a receptionist in the Council office was also good on-the-job training for when Tanya ran for the Council. She had already learned which members always voted no, which ones were vulnerable and which ones were untouchable in an election. She hoped that in two or three years, she'd be in a solid position to make her first run. And part of solidifying that position was making a positive impression on both the voting members of the tribe and the Council itself now, although she hated to qualify her good deeds in such a selfish way. She was making a dent—that was what really counted.

Still, Nick's presence had complicated things—and that was putting it mildly. She'd never been able to say no to him, so the fact that she hadn't let him kiss her the other night was, well, weird. Tanya was proud of herself for not letting Nick charm her into something she would regret. She was sticking to her guns. It made her feel surprisingly grown-up.

But she also felt terrible, and she wasn't exactly sure why. Nick *was* trying—in his materialistic kind of way—and she felt as if she was slamming every door in his face. She wanted to be glad to see him. She wanted to be happy he was interested in their son. She desperately wanted something good to come out of this. What, she didn't know. Maybe that was the problem.

The emcee called for all dancers to line up for the opening dance. Tanya slow-walked Bear to the end of the line, where he tried to grab the jingle cones off the dress in front of him. Everyone laughed, and Tanya had a moment of profound peace with the situation. She belonged here, and so did Bear. This place, these traditions, these people—they were a part of her. She wouldn't turn her back on them.

The emcee was in the middle of the opening prayer when Tanya felt something change, like lightning had struck nearby. She glanced around, but no one else seemed to notice the strange charge to the air.

Then she saw him. Nick Longhair was on the other side of the circle watching her. He had one boot-clad foot on the lowest rung of the fence, and an expensive-looking cowboy hat tipped back on his head. The jeans were dark, the T-shirt was tight and the belt buckle shone in the sunlight. He looked like the old Nick, dressed up fancy for a big date. A more expensive version of the old Nick, that was. But the sight of him was enough to make her light-headed. Not the old Nick. A better Nick.

Tanya gasped when his eyes locked on to hers. He'd come. He was really here. Or she was hallucinating, but if this was a dream, it was the best dream she could imagine. He wasn't so ashamed of his heritage that he wouldn't even put in an appearance at a powwow. He wasn't so ashamed of her that he wouldn't be seen in public with her.

The drumming started, and the line began to move into the dance circle. Nick stayed where he was. A few people came up to talk to him, and from what Tanya could see as she and the other dancers moved around the circle, Nick was being friendly instead of standoff-ish. He shook hands and slapped the backs of a couple of guys who Tanya recognized as old classmates. He even seemed to smile as people pointed to his short hair. He didn't look resentful or act like he was here against his will. Maybe he was faking it—she wouldn't put it past him, not after she'd seen the look of horror on his face when she'd suggested he come to the powwow in the first place. But if he was faking it, at least he had the decency to fake it well.

Finally, the opening dance ended. Nick had moved around to the entrance to wait for them. "Hiya, Tanya." He had the gall to tip his hat.

That irritating light-headedness got less light. She could feel the pressure of dozens of eyeballs boring into her back. Everyone knew they'd once been an item. Everyone knew she had a child. As far as everyone knew, Nick didn't know about Bear until this very moment.

Clearly, everyone was waiting for a scene.

Tanya was frozen. She should do something—what, exactly, eluded her—but she couldn't even open her mouth. Nick didn't jump into the gap either. He stood with his hands on his hips, a smile that was more of a challenge than a greeting on his face. *Your move,* his dancing eyes seemed to say to her. But she had no move to make.

Good Lord, the whole crowd of people around them was silent. The drummers weren't even drumming, which meant there was no sound to drown out the pounding of her heart. She didn't have a plan B. Hell, she wasn't sure she had a plan A, unless passing out from confusion was a plan. If it was, it wasn't a good one, that much she knew.

Bear was the one who broke the tension, God bless the boy. He began clapping and waving at Nick, clearly remembering the nice man who came with toys. "Hi, guy," Nick said as he plopped his cowboy hat down on Bear's small head.

A good-natured chuckle passed through the crowd, the drummers picked up the next drumbeat and the powwow moved on.

Tanya didn't, though. Dumbstruck, she couldn't do much more than keep a grip on Bear. Part of her brain noted that this particular reaction probably meshed well with the fallacy that Nick hadn't seen the boy before. But mostly she was relieved that the spotlight had shifted off her.

"I can't believe you came." Dang it all, her voice came out quiet and wobbly.

"I think I was invited," was all the response she got.

They couldn't keep standing here. Even if the crowd wasn't collectively holding their breaths, people were still watching—and waiting for something to happen.

"Um, Mom's got a spot this way, if you want to come say hi."

"I'd love to see Doreen." Again, there was that sincerity that Tanya wasn't sure was entirely sincere. Still, it was something to do that moved them away from the crowd, so Tanya headed back to where Mom had spread out her picnic blanket and set up folding chairs. The spot was tucked away on the north side of the dance circle, underneath a pair of scrawny pine trees that provided little shade.

Mom sat in one of the chairs, fanning her face with a folded paper plate. It wasn't that hot. Tanya's mortification veered off into concern. Mom's headaches were getting worse and worse.

However, when she saw Tanya and Nick heading straight for her, Mom sat up and managed a pleasant smile. Of course, Mom knew that Nick was Bear's father. Tanya couldn't have kept that secret from her own mother if she'd tried. "Nick Longhair, as I live and breathe!"

Tanya couldn't help sighing. Mom was going to do this over-the-top. She loved her mother, she really did, but she didn't see how Mom's reaction would make this situation less awkward.

"Hello, Doreen. How are you doing?" Nick walked over and put his arm around her shoulders. "It's great to see you."

Tanya looked around, noting how many people were keeping tabs on the situation. Only fifteen or so. Not everyone, but enough that the gossips would find plenty of firsthand accounts.

"Missed seeing you around," Mom said, pulling off a good, stern tone as she looked at Bear.

"I think I'll be around a lot more now." Nick's voice

was smooth as he took Bear from Tanya's arms. He tickled the baby under the chin, then tossed him up in the air. Bear threw his arms and legs out, the wide smile on his face as loud as any scream of delight.

Was that his real, sincere answer—or was he just telling Mom what she wanted to hear? Tanya so much wanted to believe that he meant it, but she couldn't forget what he'd said just the other night—he'd be here for a year at least. Sure, he'd be around a lot more—for a year. But after that?

Would Nick get tired of playing at being an Indian again, or worse, tired of playing daddy, and hightail it back to Chicago the first chance he got?

It almost didn't matter what the answer was. As Tanya watched, he sat cross-legged on the blanket and let Bear take his hat on and off his head while keeping up a polite, friendly conversation with Mom. Every so often, Nick would glance up at Tanya and give her the kind of warm smile that made her want to melt.

Maybe it didn't matter that he would leave, which she was certain he would do. Maybe all that mattered was that he was here now.

"So you watch Bear during the day?"

"Monday through Friday," Doreen said. "We have a good ol' time, me and my Bear—don't we, sweetie?" She leaned over and touched Bear on the nose. "We watch some cartoons, make some lunch, play some games—Nana's house is always fun, isn't it, baby?"

Nick was sure Tanya had said Bear was partially deaf, but as far as he could tell, the little boy understood the vast majority of what was said to him. Right now, for example, he was stretching his arms up to Doreen as if to agree that yes, they did have loads of fun together.

But beyond that, Nick was shocked by how much Tanya's mother had changed since he'd seen her last. Her weight had ballooned—not that unusual on the rez, where the only grocery store within sixty miles was a Qwik-E Mart. However, Doreen's weight seemed to congregate in her legs, to the point that she couldn't get shoes on her feet.

How did she keep up with Bear when she could hardly walk? That worried Nick, but not as much as the way Doreen's glassy eyes blinked at different speeds. The woman looked like she was in the middle of the world's worst migraine.

"How have you been feeling?" he asked cautiously.

"Oh, you know," Doreen replied, casually waving away his concern, "we all have our crosses to carry."

Nick nodded in sympathy, but mentally, his wheels began to turn. He'd spent the last two weeks thinking about one of three things: Tanya, Bear and his current case. He was hip-deep in statements of denial from Midwest Energy Company about whether they had actually drilled underneath the Dakota River and onto the Red Creek Reservation for natural gas, and even if they had—which they were not admitting in a court of law— they were sure the chemicals used in hydraulic fracturing, or fracking, wouldn't have polluted anything.

But other evidence showed that those chemicals were showing up in groundwater. When that groundwater made it into homes, people were being poisoned, one glass of water at a time.

Nick had already checked the maps. Tanya's little house was several miles outside the radius the tribe maintained was polluted. Doreen's house was right in the middle of it.

Most medical studies of the chemical pollutants

talked about the neurological problems that occurred when people drank contaminated water. Nick was still working his way through the accusations by the tribe and the denials by Midwest. Now, however, he began to think that he needed to spend more time investigating the human impact of the pollution.

Doreen and Bear just might turn out to be the keys to his case. He just had to prove that Doreen's water was contaminated and that both she and Bear were sick because of it. And if he could tie the hearing and speech problems of an innocent child directly to the actions of a money-grubbing corporation—well, that's when lawyers started tossing around phrases like "slam dunk" and "sure thing." When confronted with that kind of adorable evidence, corporations were much more likely to sign off on huge settlements than be labeled child poisoners. And the sooner everyone signed off on huge settlements, the sooner Nick could go back to his real life.

Even as he thought about going back to Chicago, Nick took in his surroundings. Bear had climbed into his lap and was now sucking his thumb, apparently on his way toward a nap. The sky was huge; the steady drumbeat and the whirling dancers in the nearby circle made him feel alive. Some of the guys had given him crap about cutting his hair, but no one treated him like an outsider—not to his face anyway. Despite his earlier concerns about coming to the powwow, he was having fun. Fun had been the last thing on his mind when he'd made his decision. He'd only come to prove Tanya wrong, but he had the sinking feeling he'd actually proved her right.

He was going to go back to his life in Chicago, that was a given. Things here were worse than ever—at least all he'd had to worry about when drinking the water from the river as a kid had been getting an upset stomach. Now the water here was contaminated. Even if he wrung a huge settlement out of Midwest Energy, it still wouldn't cover the whole cost of cleanup once the legal fees were paid. And even though he had no concrete evidence, there was no doubt in his mind that Bear's health issues were directly connected to that contamination. All of which made one thing brutally clear.

He couldn't leave Bear on this rez.

He watched Tanya as she prepared to enter the circle for the women's shawl dance. She looked up to where he sat and shot him a small, private smile.

A sudden, powerful urge to take her with him all but smacked him between the eyes. He shook it off, though. They'd had this argument before. She wasn't going anywhere. She *liked* this hellhole. Sure, the sky here was pretty, and yeah, he was glad he'd come, but he didn't want to *live* here. A man couldn't survive on sweeping vistas alone. He had grown fond of his spacious condo, fine-dining choices and sailing on Lake Michigan. He didn't want to go back to polluted water and cardboard-covered windows.

No use getting ahead of himself. Before he started game-planning how Doreen and Bear fit into his case against Midwest Energy, he had to have his facts straight, which meant that he had to get some hard evidence that Doreen Rattling Blanket's water was contaminated and that Doreen's and Bear's health problems were tied to that. He'd need water samples and health records. And if it turned out he was right about this, then those same facts would be what he needed to win a custody battle.

He didn't want it to come to that. He didn't even want to be thinking about dragging Tanya into court. But no matter what a custody case would do to her—or his reputation back in Chicago—he refused to leave Bear in a situation where his health was in danger. This was about his son, first and foremost.

He'd have to go around Tanya. If she realized what connections he was making and what he intended to do with those connections, she might panic. He'd seen that before, too—people did stupid things when they felt cornered. He'd just found his son—he didn't want Tanya to up and disappear with the boy. No, this situation required the utmost discretion.

By the end of the day, Nick had a plan. Now he just needed an opportunity, and he got one handed to him on a silver platter. Bear was fussy—or so Nick assumed. He hadn't figured how hard it would be to understand a kid who didn't make any noise. The boy was wriggling and flopping and scowling and no matter what Tanya did, it only got worse.

"I need to take him home. He's super cranky."

Doreen looked around. "The closing dance…well, if he needs to go, we'll go."

Nick heard the disappointment in Doreen's voice and jumped at his chance. "I can take you home later, if you want to stay."

Doreen rewarded him with a huge grin. "Really? You'd do that for me?"

Her joy was so real that Nick almost felt bad for having ulterior motives. "Of course—if it's okay with Tanya, that is." They both turned to Tanya.

Nick didn't like the look on her face because it was the same look he'd been seeing a lot—one of optimism and hope mixed with a healthy dose of skepticism. Was she on to him, or was this just more of what he had coming?

"Sure," she said slowly. "That would be great." It didn't sound great, but he took it.

Tanya kissed her mom goodbye, and then Nick carried Bear back to Tanya's rust bucket of a car. Nick recognized it as the same car Doreen had been driving years ago. "This still runs, huh?"

Tanya was silent for a moment, leaving Nick to wonder if he'd managed to insult her again. But then she said, "Yup. At least I don't have to worry about Bear trashing it, you know? Not like that car of yours." Her tone was light, but not suspicious. Perfect.

"Hey, no big deal. And I got a vehicle we can put the car seat in, just so you know."

Tanya looked up at him through wary eyes. "Bought a new car, did you?"

"Actually, it's an F-250 extended-cab truck. Figured I'd need something to handle winter weather sooner or later," he added, so she wouldn't think he'd bought a truck just for child transportation reasons.

Tanya sighed, her shoulders drooping down. "I can't get used to you throwing money around, Nick. I just can't."

That he understood. It had taken several years for him to get to the point where he bought things for the fun of it instead of stuffing the money under a mattress like a squirrel hoarding nuts for the winter. "I want to see you again."

"Me or Bear?"

No, she didn't trust him. "Both. You have a standing invitation to come to my place. I bought a toddler bed for Bear and everything, so you wouldn't even have to pack."

"Where would I sleep?" She asked it carefully, as

if she knew exactly what sort of detonator was on that bomb of a question.

If they were back in her little house instead of in the parking lot of a powwow, he'd kiss her. Hell, he was thinking about kissing her anyway, but he was pretty sure he'd get punched for his trouble. He'd undoubtedly stirred up an epic hornets' nest by showing up at all, let alone spending the afternoon playing with Bear. People were going to figure out he was Bear's father sooner or later, but sooner didn't have to be this instant.

So he leaned back even as he kept his eyes locked on hers. "Babe, you may sleep wherever you want."

"Oh," was all the answer he got, but the way her cheeks colored up with a beautiful pink told him plenty. No, she didn't have to love him. He didn't have to love her either. It wasn't a strict requirement. But she still wanted him.

Luckily, the feeling was mutual.

Seven

Tanya had Bear tucked under the blankets in record time. The poor boy was exhausted. With all the excitement at the powwow, he'd missed his nap and passed out in his car seat before she'd made it half a mile down the road.

She was almost as tired, but she didn't think she was in danger of falling asleep anytime soon. Nick's words still waltzed around her mind, spinning her in tighter and tighter circles.

Want. That was the word her brain was stuck on. He'd asked her if she still wanted him. He'd told her she could sleep anywhere she wanted. He wasn't asking her to do anything she didn't want.

So what did she want?

What seemed like a simple question made her so dizzy that she had to hold on to the sides of the shower while she rinsed her hair. Nick had shown up at the powwow. And he'd been correct—she'd *asked* him to go. But she hadn't thought he actually would come. She still couldn't believe it. In fact, she didn't. She'd just dreamed that Nick had sat with her mother and played with their son, his eyes always watching Tanya. She'd imagined that he had publicly acknowledged Bear—well, not *acknowledged*. As far as she knew, he hadn't told anyone he was Bear's father. But he'd publicly accepted the boy in a drama-free way, which was practically the same thing. And if that wasn't good enough, he'd even driven Mom home. Tanya hadn't been so sure that Mom would be glad to see Nick, but he'd managed to win her over. The day had been so perfect that she wished she'd taken a picture of it to make it last longer.

It bordered on too-good-to-be-true. The only thing she couldn't reconcile was the Nick who had shown up today with the Nick who had flinched in horror a few days earlier at the mention of the powwow. She couldn't shake the feeling that Nick was doing a damn fine job of faking his sincerity.

Maybe she was overthinking this. She had been known to do that, after all. Maybe she'd just caught him by surprise after scraping up his dashboard. That car had to have cost him a fortune. It wasn't like he'd come here and trashed her stuff. He'd just been upset, that was all. Maybe he'd gone home and decided he wanted to come, to be a part of their lives. Maybe— just maybe—he had no other motives.

Maybe she was the one who was wrong—about him.

He's the one who left me, she tried to remind herself, but the thought rang hollow. She was digging deep for some excuse to throw up between them. Too deep. That thought felt like a desperate avoidance of a reality she couldn't bring herself to grasp. What had he said, back during the fight in his office? That she didn't believe he could've given her what she wanted? What had he meant by that? She'd always known he could be anything he'd wanted—and he'd done nothing but prove her right. He'd wanted to be the smartest, richest man in the tribe, with the nicest things. Isn't that exactly what he'd done? Why he'd left her behind?

Unless she had it wrong. He'd seemed hurt—and not a calculated, intentional hurt. He'd acted like *she'd* rejected *him*. How was that even possible? It wasn't, unless… A new idea cropped up. Maybe Nick hadn't left her just because he wanted to be rich. Maybe he had another reason for leaving and not coming back until now.

She didn't know what that reason could be, but the realization that there could be another side to the story had her questioning her entire position. What if, instead of her being the wronged woman, he had been the wronged man? "In fact," she remembered him saying, "if I recall correctly, I asked you to come with me." Had he really? Or was he just remembering things to his advantage?

Tanya squeezed the water out of her hair and slipped the light cotton nightie over her head. She was *way* overthinking things. It was late, she was tired and obviously, her mind was spinning out of control. She should just get some sleep. There was bound to be more clarity in the morning.

She padded to the kitchen to get a drink of water and some aspirin. She was getting old—well, older, anyway—and a day spent dancing in thin-soled moccasins on uneven ground meant that her feet were going to be sore for a few days.

She was putting the glass into the sink when she

heard it. *Tap, tap.* She froze, her ears straining, but she'd know that sound anywhere.

Tap. Tap.

Someone was knocking on a window with an index finger. And only one person knocked like that.

Nick had come.

Her heart began to pound in what felt like a highly irregular clip, probably because she couldn't tell if she was excited or terrified. She was in her jammies, her hair still damp from the shower. This wasn't exactly putting her best foot forward.

But more than that, Nick's intention was obvious. He wasn't here for some quality father-son bonding time. Tapping on her windows after he knew Bear had already been tired? That could only mean one thing.

Nick had come for her.

Tap. Tap.

Suddenly, she was kicking herself. She hadn't gotten any condoms. First off, she hadn't exactly had the opportunity to pick up some. But more than that, she'd told herself she didn't need any—she was not being charmed into anything by Nick. Not yesterday, not today and most certainly not tomorrow. No scratching of Nick-sized itches allowed.

Except that had all changed tonight. All of the arguments she'd had—*good* arguments for keeping Nick out of her bed and, to a certain extent, out of her life— seemed unfounded after today. More than ever before, he'd been everything she'd wanted.

Tap. Tap.

The final round of tapping snapped her out of her paralysis. Still not entirely sure what she wanted to happen next, she hurried to the front window.

Nick stood there, straddling the lone clump of black-eyed Susans that Tanya had managed to keep alive. When she peeked through the blind, she saw the worried look on his face. Goodness, she'd taken so long that he'd thought she wasn't coming. Then he raised his finger to tap again and saw her.

Even through the glass and the blinds, she felt the full heat of his smile. He pulled his hand back and tilted his head to where his big, shiny truck was a shadow behind him.

Two long years of sheer sexual frustration slammed her low in the belly. No, it was more than that. True, she'd been with Nick two years ago—she had the son to prove it—but one wild night had barely made a dent in the backlog she'd accumulated in the previous two years. That meant she just had one night with Nick in the whole of four long years.

It wasn't enough. She had to have been nuts to think it had been, because right now, she felt more than a little crazy.

She opened the door. She had to move slowly to keep the door from squeaking. Life is funny, she thought. Two years ago, she'd done the same thing, but then it had been to keep from waking her mother. Now she was desperate not to wake up her son. The rough concrete of her stoop was cool underneath her feet, but the sensation was enough to let her know she was not dreaming this. Not by a long shot.

Nick stood at the bottom of the three steps, one foot propped up on the bottom step. He still had on his hat, but it was tipped way back on his head. The dim gleam of moonlight caught his eyes under the brim, and Tanya would have sworn they shone with the same aching desire that she felt.

"I got a truck," he said, his voice pitched low.

That's what he had always said, all the times before when he'd tapped on her window in the middle of the night. True, it wasn't quite three in the morning—more like ten-thirty—but Tanya felt that she was lost in the past and surging through the present at the same time. Who knew what the future held?

Nick's eyes skimmed over her bare legs and lingered on her chest. "Wanna go for a ride?" he added, and she heard the strain in his voice. She suddenly got the sense that he didn't know what her answer was going to be. He didn't consider her a sure thing anymore, but he wanted her enough to ask and keep asking.

Another part of her reserve melted. He'd always said that, too, and in that second, Tanya wasn't the conflicted, tired mom, but the wild-in-love girl she'd always been. And Nick? He was the same boy she'd loved since she was twelve. Nothing had changed. It never would, she saw now.

Nick held his hand out to her. It wasn't too late. She could still say no—if she wanted.

What did she want?

For the second time that day, she was struck dumb by Nick's sudden appearance. How could he be the same boy she'd always loved but also this man who she wasn't sure she understood?

He took one step up. One step closer. "We don't have to go anywhere. I know you can't leave Bear..." He cleared his throat. "Just tell me what you want, Tanya. If you want me to go, I'll go." Another step up. Now they were eye to eye, close enough that Tanya could feel Nick's body heat through her thin nightie. His hand circled around her waist, pulling her in. His chest was firm against hers—strong where she was weak. He leaned his forehead against hers, and even that simple touch had her melting. "Tell me what you want, babe."

What did she want? What she'd always wanted. "You won't leave me?"

He shook his head, a slow, deliberate movement that told her this wasn't some knee-jerk answer. "I'll stay all night if you want, babe."

All night. Not forever. A small, insistent part of her vigorously shouted that his answer wasn't good enough. She wanted him not just for now, but for always, and she'd settle for nothing less.

But then her heart—and her body—overruled that dissenting thought. She loved him; at the very least, he cared for her, much more than anyone else ever had. She had a Nick-sized itch dying to be scratched. Her body ached for the release that only Nick could give her.

Then he kissed her. His tongue swept over her lips and then through them, scratching that itch at the same time it drove it deeper underneath her skin. Oh, how she'd dreamed of this moment, having Nick back in her arms. Whatever resolve she had left wilted under the direct heat of his kiss. He had come back for her, just like she'd wanted.

She threw her arms around his neck and tangled her fingers in his short hair as she kissed him back. The freedom of the choice unexpectedly took her desire from a dull ache to a searing pain—but a good pain, the kind that left a woman stronger on the other side. She crushed her body against Nick's, trying to remember every sensation, every touch—just in case she had to wait another two years for the next time. He might leave her in the morning, or when his case was done, but she knew now that there would always be a next time. He would always come back to her.

Suddenly, with her implicit approval, Nick took the kiss deeper. The last two years fell away as his hands left their heated mark on her back, her hips, her bottom. Then he was pulling at the edge of her nightie, pulling it higher and higher.

As quickly as it had come on, her desire dropped off a high cliff. She untangled her hands from his hair and jerked her hem away from him. "Don't."

He pulled back in confusion, and she mentally kicked herself. The first thing she could come up with was "don't"? How utterly lame. Maybe this wasn't a good idea. Maybe it was a really, *really* bad one.

"Why not?" Nick was all but panting, and she could feel the straining bulge below his belt buckle. Despite that, his tone was careful and hardly disappointed at all.

"Because—well—" She forced herself to take a deep breath and try again. "Because I'm not the same girl I used to be." That girl had had a different body. She was embarrassed at how ashamed she was of her post-baby body. It was killing the mood.

A funny smile crossed Nick's face, and the next thing Tanya knew, he'd swept her right off her feet and was carrying her to his truck. In seconds, he had set her down on the lowered tailgate. Then, with great deliberation, he stepped between her legs.

So maybe she hadn't killed the mood—hadn't even dented it, because that bulge below his buckle rubbed against her bare flesh and threw her right back into that needy place where only Nick had the answers. Then, his eyes locked on to hers, he lifted her nightie up and free of her. The shock of being completely naked before him in the back of a truck jolted Tanya even harder against that bulge. Even though his face didn't change, she heard the low groan come from deep in his throat.

"The girl I used to know," he began as his hands settled on her shoulders, "liked this." He lifted her still-damp hair to one side and leaned down, tracing the tip of his tongue against the edge of her ear with the barest hint of pressure.

Tanya couldn't have kept back the gasp that broke loose if she'd tried. All Nick had ever needed to do was come up behind her and lick her ear. He hadn't forgotten. He remembered *her*.

"The girl I used to know," Nick went on, his voice so very low and warm in her ear, "liked this, too." Then he scraped her lobe between his teeth—not hard enough to hurt, but just hard enough to make her entire body shudder against his.

"Yes," she heard herself whisper. She'd loved that feeling of being devoured, of being so delicious and special. That hadn't changed, not even a little bit. She wanted him to consume her. She ran her hands through his hair again, feeling how different the short was from the long of her memory. Right now, it didn't feel like a personal attack on his heritage. In fact, it wasn't getting in the way, but left her plenty to hold on to. Maybe she didn't hate his new hair. She rubbed her cheek against it, feeling the ends tickle her skin. Maybe she liked it— hard to tell, though, what with Nick sucking on her ear and rubbing her shoulders and pressing that hard bulge against her. Hell, she did like it. She liked it *all*.

"The girl I used to know liked this, too." Nick's mouth moved down, where he nipped at the spot where her neck met her shoulder. Then his body was pushing her back until she had to brace herself with one hand so she didn't tip over. Nick's hot mouth closed around her left nipple, those teeth scraping along with the just-right amount of pressure to drive her wild. His other arm wrapped around her waist to hold her steady while he nibbled and licked and sucked on her breast like it was dinnertime and she was the main course.

"Yes, oh, yes," she heard herself saying over and over. Nick switched to the other breast, but instead of continuing to hold her up, one of his hands caressed around the side of her waist and down her thigh. He lifted her leg up and wrapped it around his waist, which caused her other leg to do the same all by itself. When she had him firmly within her grasp, he leaned forward, driving that bulge against her opening center. "Oh!"

A deep, guttural noise moved up from deep in his chest until his mouth vibrated around her wet skin. "The girl I used to know," he murmured against her, the heat from his body pushing away the light chill of the night sky, "liked everything about this."

He leaned back long enough to strip off his T-shirt. Instantly, Tanya's hands were all over him, feeling the new, harder planes of his chest. He stood, with his eyes closed and his chest heaving, as she discovered him all over again. He hadn't so much grown *up* as he'd grown *into* a man. Still the same, but different. He looked like he was hanging on to his self-control by the thinnest of strings. If she recalled correctly, there were a few things that he liked, too. She gave one of his nipples a tweak, just to see what would happen.

He gasped and staggered forward so hard that he had to prop himself up with his hands to keep from falling on top of her. "Tanya," he hissed out between clenched teeth. That made her smile. He might have reduced her to a quivering mess, but she knew all his triggers, too. She leaned up and bit him just above the nipple—not too hard, but hard enough to leave a red mark. She could leave her mark on him after all. She already had—she just hadn't been able to see it until this moment.

The groan that escaped his mouth seemed to thrum through her body all the way down to where his buckle was standing between them. She couldn't hold back much longer. Two years. Her mind kept rolling over and over the words—two years since she'd had this moment. All she could do was pray that she wouldn't have to wait another two years before she could have him again. She made a grab at his buckle—she was damnably tired of that disc of metal coming between them—but he caught her hands and pushed them away as he made a clucking noise. "The girl I used to know always was a little impatient."

She could hear the teasing in his tone, but there was no mistaking the way his voice was rough with the same need that made her so greedy.

Nick undid his buckle and shucked his pants down. He sprang free of his clothes, his length rising to meet her center. But when he leaned forward, Tanya pulled back. Yes, she was stupid-crazy for him. But she couldn't afford to pay the price a second time around. "Wait."

"'S okay," he mumbled as he clawed at his now-fallen jeans. Long seconds later, he pulled a small plastic square out of his back pocket. He rolled the condom on while Tanya shivered without his touch to keep her warm. As soon as he was protected, he leaned back into her. "I missed you so much, babe."

"I missed you, too." Talking was harder than she thought it would be. Her throat was all clogged up with relief and desire and emotions she couldn't even name. She wanted to tell him more than that—how much she needed him, how she would always love him no matter what.

But those words died on her tongue the moment he entered her. Her body convulsed so hard that she couldn't do anything but hold on to him. "Nick," she managed to say. But that was all.

It wasn't as if she had forgotten what sex with Nick was like, because she hadn't. Rare was the day when she didn't think about—dream about—the nights they drove off in a truck and had sex under the stars.

But she *had* forgotten. Time had dulled the sensation of Nick filling her, of Nick kissing her, of Nick loving her. Because he did. She could feel it in the way he stroked into her—hard, like she'd always liked it, but not violently. She could tell by how he couldn't keep his hands off her, and by how he kept kissing her and then kissing her some more.

For a shining moment, Tanya forgot about the past two years, and the two years before that. She forgot about the Council and the job, her mother and her son. She forgot about wanting to make a difference and wanting a better life. All she could think about was how she had loved this man since she'd known what love was. This wasn't just sex. This was *making* love.

She gave him everything she had. Everything. She couldn't hold back—what if? But Nick pushed those thoughts far from her mind. Still thrusting, he moved down until he was licking her breasts again while he held her up. All Tanya could do was dig her fingers into his hair and hold on for the ride.

Suddenly, Nick's mouth relinquished its hold on her nipples. He crushed her up into his chest, surrounding her with his strong arms. "Babe," he managed to get out as he drove harder and harder into her.

Tanya's world exploded around her, the force of the unleashed orgasm obliterating everything but Nick. Nick. She couldn't even say his name, but she didn't have to. With a low roar and a final series of thrusts, he came.

He still loved her. He hadn't forgotten her.

He pulled out, leaving Tanya feeling empty and a little lost. He'd promised he wouldn't leave, but what if...

She shouldn't have worried, though. Nick buckled up, handed her the nightie and then climbed up onto the tailgate with her. It was only then that Tanya noticed the sleeping bags behind her. He'd thought of everything, but they hadn't even made it all the way into the truck bed. That's what two years of frustration did, she figured with a smile.

Nick crawled back onto the sleeping bags and patted the space next to him. Happier than she wanted to admit, Tanya took her place beside him and was rewarded with his arms pulling her into a monster hug.

"You're right," he murmured into her hair. "You're not the girl I used to know."

"Oh?" That was all she could say. She had no idea if she should be terrified or what.

He kissed her on the temple and then sighed—a sound of total satisfaction. "You're something even better. The woman I know now."

Eight

Nick waited for Tanya to say something. He knew she would—sooner or later anyway—but he didn't know what it would be. He would have guessed that she'd go all sentimental on him and tell him she loved him. That should have scared the hell out of him. But now that they were here, curled up in the back of his truck, the smell of sex still clinging to the air around them, the thought didn't bother him as much.

However, he didn't want to jump into the void either. Mostly because he didn't know what he would say next. His heart was still racing and his mind felt both fogged-up and crystal clear at the same time. What he was mostly thinking about was the weight of Tanya's warm body curled against him, how he could feel the fluttering of her heartbeat against his skin and the way her fingers traced a path between his still-bare chest, his face and his hair. Especially that. In fact, if she kept it up, he'd have to get that second condom out of the glove box.

He had always remembered the sex as being incredible, but somehow, this had been beyond the scope of that simple word. *More,* he found himself thinking. More than just sex. Something much more.

And Tanya had been worried he wouldn't like her body? That idea was so ridiculous as to be laughable. Yeah, the curves were different than what he remembered. That wasn't a bad thing, though. In fact, it was a very, *very* good thing. The swell of her hips, those luscious breasts—oh, yeah, that was way *more*. Even now he was having trouble keeping his hands off her.

But he did. What she'd said he'd said—"Been good seeing you, Tanya. Have a nice life, Tanya"—ran around his head like a dog off the leash. He *didn't* remember saying that. He must have said something, though, something that hurt her. As he watched the stars and stroked her hair, he found himself struggling to think what it could have been.

The minutes passed unaccounted for. He didn't know what time it was, and he didn't care. This—being here with Tanya, in the back of a truck, under the stars—had been a homecoming more important to him than just setting foot on the rez. He felt like he'd rediscovered a part of him that he had lost. Well, not lost, but forgotten. He'd forgotten how free being with Tanya could make him feel. Right now, he truly felt at home, and he didn't want to do anything to ruin that.

It had to end. Even he knew that. He had no interest in spending the night in the back of this truck. Soon enough, Tanya's chest rose and fell in an extra-heavy sigh. Here it comes, he thought.

"What happens next?" Her voice was soft, all the

contentious edges wiped clean. She sounded sexier than she ever had without the benefit of actual pillow talk. Of course, they didn't have any actual pillows. The truck was nice in a sentimental sense, but a bed would be better.

He wouldn't hurt her again. So he chose his words carefully as he gave her another squeeze. "This is what I'd like to happen, but I want to hear what you want, too."

"Oh." She didn't so much say the word as exhale it against his skin. "Okay."

He braced himself for the potential tempest he was about to unleash in the back of a truck. "I'd like for you and Bear to spend the weekend with me—every weekend. Bear has his own room at my place."

"And I can sleep wherever I want, right?" As she said it, she traced a lazy circle on his chest.

How many condoms did he have in the glove box? Two more, he remembered. He'd left the rest of the box at home, counting on her arrival. "Anywhere." He had to grab her hand to stop the circle before all the clarity evaporated and left him with nothing but fog. Then he waited to see what she'd say.

"Okay."

Okay? That was it? No push back, no argument? He asked, she agreed? It had to be a first. Feeling bold, he pressed on. "I'd also like to have dinner with you—and Bear—a few nights a week. Help out around the house if you want me to, that sort of thing. Just spend some time with you both."

"Yeah?" The disbelief was barely noticeable, but he still heard it.

He weighed his options. Yes, he could demand his parental rights or tell her he was getting Bear tested no matter what, but that felt unnecessary. What this particular situation called for was reassurances. "Look, babe, there's no need for the courts to get involved. This isn't a custody issue, as far as I'm concerned. Bear belongs with you. But I want to be a part of his life—of your life. I want to take him to the doctor's, pick him up from your mom's and just, you know, get to *know* him." They could deal with the possible contamination later. Arguing with Tanya right now did not make for good pillow talk.

"For how long?"

Despite the warm glow, despite feeling free, despite the beautiful woman in his arms, he bristled. He was trying to be reassuring, and she still treated him like he was the enemy. He sat up, scooting away from her until his feet hit the ground and he had a hold of his shirt. The flash of anger had erased nearly all the good feelings he'd been basking in. She wanted to push? Fine. It was high time he did a little pushing back of his own.

"Look, I am *sorry* I didn't call you back. I truly am. But you keep acting as if I willfully hung you and Bear out to dry, and that's not what happened. I know you think I bailed on you—which I did *not*—but if you think that I'm going to walk out on my own son like a callous, heartless bastard, then maybe *you* should get out of the back of *my* truck."

Immediately, he wished he'd kept his big, fat mouth shut. Her face dropped so fast that she looked like he'd backhanded her. "Tanya—"

"What I want, because you actually *bothered* to ask," she said, her voice cold and level as she climbed out of the truck with more grace than he'd managed, "is to know which Nick I'm dealing with—the one I loved, or the one who left. That's what I want. I thought, after today…" The pain in her voice was raw, and for the first time, he realized exactly how much she was hurting. Nick reached for her, but she danced away from him. "You act like I drove you away," she went on, each word a bullet that sliced through the air, "like you already blame me for driving you away the next time. Because there will always be a next time. I already know you're going to break my heart, Nick. It's what you do." He opened his mouth to defend himself, but she wasn't done yet. "You want to hear the sad thing? No matter how many times you break it, I'll still love you." She turned on her heel.

Now it was his turn to feel like he'd been slapped, and hard. "No, wait. Tanya, wait!" This time, he didn't let her get away. He grabbed her arm and spun her around until they were face-to-face. "Did you mean that? That you still love me?"

"Of course I do," she replied, rubbing at her eyes with the back of her free hand. "I never stopped. I only wish…" she sniffed, but went on "…I wish you felt the same, that's all. Now let me *go*."

For an agonizing second, he couldn't move, couldn't think. Her words made perfect sense, but at the same time they confused everything. Nick crushed her to his chest, his mouth taking savage possession of hers. Tanya made a guttural noise of protest, but Nick wasn't letting her push him away this time. He'd promised himself that he wouldn't leave her hurting again. Now was the time to prove it to her.

"I will never let you go," he whispered in her ear before he kissed his way down her neck. "I never did."

Her chest rose in a ragged sob. For the life of him, Nick had no idea if Tanya crying was a good thing or not—as far as he could remember, she'd never broken down before. Not around him anyway.

Then she ran her fingers through his hair and pulled his head up to hers. "How can I trust you? How can I believe you won't run back to Chicago the first chance you get?" Tears streamed down her cheeks. She made it sound as if he would tuck tail and run, like some sort of coward. As if he would just bail on his son. As if he would bail on her. He didn't know how they'd make things work, long distance, but he knew now that he couldn't *not* have her in his life. He couldn't forget this part of himself again.

"I can't, babe." Her face started to fall again, but he didn't give her the chance to bolt on him again. He rubbed away her tears with his thumbs. "I have to show you. Will you let me do that?" He tilted her head back until he could look her in the eye. "Let me show you."

"Okay," she half whispered, half sobbed, but at least this time, she had a happy little smile to go with it.

The kiss this time was different—not one fueled by desperation or need. Instead, it felt like the kind of intimacy, the closeness, that he'd never felt with any other woman. Rissa had never given him this feeling of, well, *love*. Tanya loved him. She'd never stopped loving him.

He considered lifting her back up into the truck bed, but that seemed...wrong. Like it was a moment in their past that they'd moved beyond. They weren't the same crazy kids anymore. Even though they'd just done so, making love in the back of a truck suddenly seemed too juvenile.

"One second," he murmured before he disentangled himself from her arms. He hurried to the cab of the truck and fished the two remaining condoms out of the glove box. Then he came back and picked Tanya up—she was standing barefoot in the middle of her front yard, after all.

She didn't fight him or even ask him what he was doing. She clung to his neck as he carried her up to the house, opened the door for him and shut it behind him. Only then did he set her down, on the couch.

"Wait," she said as she slipped out of his grasp.

He watched her silent figure pad back to the bedroom. She was checking on Bear, he realized. She wasn't gone long. A few moments later, he heard the sound of the bedroom door shutting, then she appeared, a vision of perfect womanhood. All those womanly curves underneath the sweet white nightgown, the intent, happy look on her face—"Perfect," he heard himself say. And he meant it. She *was* perfect for him.

Her mouth twisted in a pleased smile, then she pulled her nightgown off for the second time tonight. This time, she didn't show the slightest bit of self-consciousness as she straddled him and pulled his belt free of his jeans. Already, he was straining behind his zipper, the intensity of his need stoked by her fingers working on loosening the denim.

He groaned as she took the condom from him and rolled it on. Any clarity he'd had disappeared beneath the exquisite fog caused by Tanya's hands moving up and down his length, and then the rush that came when she settled her body on top of his. "Oh, *babe*."

Then he couldn't help himself. He buried his face in her breasts, kissing and nibbling and licking every single part of them while she moved up and down, back and forth. And the sounds she made—quiet gasps, low moans—those were for his ears only. She was for him only.

"I missed you so much," she whispered as she sank

down onto him again and again and again. "Missed...
you."

Still sucking on one of her nipples, Nick let his hands
move over her back, down to her bottom and over her
hips. *Perfect,* he thought again. Her new, generous pro-
portions gave him so much more to hold, and to hold
on to.

He pulled her down hard, and then harder, loving
each little noise she made as their bodies rocked in
unison. "I need you." And the weird thing was, he was
actively having her—but it only made him need her
more. *More.* That's what she was. That's what this was.
More than a smart career move, more than relieving a
little tension, more than any of the games that went on
in Chicago. This wasn't a game at all. This was real.

She had her hands buried in his hair, holding his head
right where he wanted it. The tempo picked up, driving
him right to the edge. He grabbed her bottom, pulling
her even farther apart so that he could drive in deeper
and deeper. She gasped, and for a second he was afraid
he'd gone too hard, too fast—but then she hissed, *"Yes,"*
as everything about her tightened down. That was all
he needed. Pumping furiously, he exploded into her.

Suddenly, Nick was tired. Exhausted. His head and
arms felt heavier than they ever had. He'd given her everything he had, and he knew good and well that she'd
done the same, but it had left him with very little clarity
and a whole bunch of warm, happy fog. His head rolled
back onto the couch, and he looked up at her.

He wanted to stay. A part of him wanted this—her—
for a long time. Maybe forever. But his life wasn't so
simple that he could throw away everything he'd worked
for, everything he'd accomplished, just because he

might be in love with the mother of his son. That's not how his world worked anymore.

That was a big enough problem. The bigger problem was that Tanya didn't realize it. "Love you," she whispered, her voice so soft that he felt it more than heard it.

He needed to say something, but it had to be the right thing. Nothing that would tear her down, but nothing that would build up her hopes. His mind spun in circles, waiting for the right words to appear. He was a lawyer, damn it. He ought to be able to say *something*.

Tanya leaned back, her gaze searching his as she lifted her body off him. That sadness—acceptance, really—danced around the edges of her eyes again, but she shook it off and gave him a satisfied smile. "It's okay. I understand."

He wanted to believe that, but he didn't think she did.

Nine

Something just beyond Nick's grasp shifted, like there was someone watching him. Then the smell hit him—souring milk and…biscuits? Where was he? Although his head screamed in protest, he managed to pry one eye open.

Bear's face was less than a foot from his. The little boy had both a thumb and the ear to his teddy bear crammed into his mouth, and he was wearing a Onesie. When he saw Nick's eye open, his eyes smiled for him and he threw himself at Nick's head.

"Oof," was all Nick could say as the boy climbed up and sat on him. "What time is it?"

"Seven," Tanya called from the kitchen. She sounded awake. Perky, even. "Which, you should know, is considered 'sleeping in' to a toddler."

Seven? As in, the morning? Nick shut his eye again. This had to be a bad dream. In Chicago, he spent Saturday nights out on the town and rarely got into bed much before three on Sunday mornings. If he was lucky, he got up in time for lunch. True, he hadn't been out on the town last night, but he'd exerted himself in plenty of other ways that required at least another hour of sleep. Preferably two.

Then the thin string of baby drool hit him on the cheek. "I'm up, I'm up," he mumbled, hauling Bear off his chest and sitting up. "Morning, Bear."

Bear smiled at him again, and Nick decided he didn't mind getting up early. At least everyone here was happy to see him. That hadn't always been the case when he'd spent the night with Rissa in Chicago. Then the little boy scrambled down and tottered his way back to the bedroom.

Finally, Nick got both of his eyes to focus, and he saw Tanya. Still barefoot, still in that short nightgown, her legs almost glowing in the early-morning sunlight that streamed in through the window over the sink. Her hair hung loose down her back as she stood over the stove, and Nick thought she might be humming. "Good morning," he said again. "When did you get up?" Because the last thing he remembered was falling asleep with her in his arms on the couch. The couch had been better than the truck, but it still wasn't as good as an actual bed. They were definitely going to spend the next weekend at his place.

Tanya looked at him over her shoulder and gave him a grin that was both innocent and entirely too wicked at the same time. "About forty-five minutes ago. I let you sleep. Breakfast is almost ready." She turned with a skillet in hand and the scent of sausage smacked him upside the head. Man, he was *hungry*.

Bear came back out of the bedroom pulling a ratty-looking blanket and the first book Nick had read to him, *The Very Hungry Caterpillar.*

"After breakfast, little man," Nick told him as he picked up the boy and attempted to put him in his high chair. "Food first."

A profound sense of peace overcame him. Nick hadn't expected to feel such a sense of belonging here with Tanya, nor had he expected that family life would come so naturally. Right now, he didn't have to worry about watching his back or protecting his flank from an attack. He didn't have to worry about making sure he had on the right tie or the right suit. He didn't have to worry about what people wanted from him or how far they'd go to get it. None of that mattered. The only thing that mattered to Tanya and Bear was that he was here with them. He didn't have to prove that he'd earned his place at this table. They welcomed him with open arms and wide smiles. It was simple. Easy, even.

Which is not to say that he'd forgotten everything. As he ate homemade biscuits and sausage and drank Tanya's extra-strong coffee, he began to make a mental list of everything he had to do. At the very top of that list was one action item that was a list in and of itself: he had to get Bear to a doctor. The sooner, the better.

He wanted to believe that the sense of urgency he felt about this was due only to his fatherly concern, but even he knew that wasn't the whole truth. Yes, the boy needed medical attention. Badly. Nick couldn't think of a better way to prove himself to Tanya than to take care of Bear—to give him the voice he so desperately needed.

But.

The "but" was huge because he knew that Tanya would view it as a betrayal. He needed to get Bear tested because he needed those test results for his case against Midwest Energy. He had a bottle of water he'd filled up at Doreen's house under his passenger seat. The water had smelled terrible, and Nick didn't doubt for a second that it had so much methane and diesel in it that he could have held a match to a running stream and it would have lit on fire. That was the most impressive sign that the water table had been contaminated.

That Bear and Doreen had been contaminated.

If Tanya knew about the details of the case, she would accuse Nick of using her and Bear to win. She'd get that horrible, fallen look on her face, and Nick would know he'd broken her heart again. She'd still love him—she'd said she would—but she wouldn't trust him. Not for a long time, maybe not forever. She would fight him with everything she had to make sure he didn't get to spend time with his own son.

Part of him knew he should tell her about his plans up front, which would give him the opportunity to justify his actions. But he couldn't. The case was confidential, and Tanya wasn't on the list of people who were in the know. Besides, he preferred to ask for forgiveness rather than for permission. And it's not like he was lying. He wanted Bear to get better. No matter if the test results helped or hurt his case, he'd still see the medical treatment through to the end. It's not like he was going to walk away the moment the case ended.

He was in this for the long haul.

"I want to get Bear to a doctor," he told Tanya over what turned out to be one of the best breakfasts he'd had in a long time. "Can you tell me where things stand right now?"

For the first time all morning, a look of worry crossed her face. "There's a clinic in Parkson. The doctor there did a hearing test and checked for strep throat—said sometimes strep will do this. But it wasn't strep, and he couldn't do anything else." She dropped her eyes, clearly ashamed. "He referred me to a pediatric specialist in Sioux Falls, but that doctor didn't take on patients who were on CHIP." Nick must have looked confused, because she added, "South Dakota Children's Health Insurance Program."

That made Nick mad. God, how he had hated being poor and ignored. No way he was letting that happen to his son. No *way*. "Is that even legal? Doesn't he have to take you?"

"I tried to tell them that, but they kept telling me how much money an initial visit cost, and how the tests might cost thousands, and how I had to pay that money up front before they'd even schedule the appointment..." her voice trailed off. "Dr. Klein is supposed to be the best in the state. Dr. Jawarski said so—that's the guy in Parkson. But I didn't have the money. I *don't* have the money," she corrected.

"I do. Give me the doctor's name. I'll take care of it." First, he'd rip that doctor a new one for refusing to help Bear. If they had to go out of state for attention, so be it.

"It'll cost thousands," she said, her voice small. "It's a lot of money."

"Not to me." When her head snapped up, he held out a hand. "Tanya, I know you think I'm shallow and greedy—and maybe I am—but this is the whole reason I wanted to have money. People don't ignore you when you're rich, and they don't write you off when you're powerful. You watch—I'll have an appointment for Bear within two weeks. If not sooner."

She opened her mouth again, but Nick cut her off. "And don't act like you're asking this huge favor of me and you're going to owe me, because you don't. This is the way it's going to work from now on. If Bear needs something like this, I'm going to take care of it. No negotiations, no arguments."

"That's going to take a little getting used to." But he heard how pleased she was. Good.

He reached over and cupped her cheek in his hand. "You've taken care of Bear the best you can for a whole year. Now it's my turn to take care of you—both of you."

"Okay." Again, it seemed almost too easy. Tanya agreeing with him—no negotiations, no arguments? *That* was going to take a little getting used to.

The tenderness of the moment lasted right until Bear hit Nick upside the head with a pre-chewed chunk of biscuit. Tanya started to giggle, Bear clapped his hands and Nick couldn't do anything but smile.

For the first time, he wasn't fighting for a client or the highest bidder.

For the first time, he was fighting for his family.

"No, I want to talk to Dr. Klein personally." Nick managed to keep his voice completely professional, but he was beginning to see why Tanya had given up on the specialist. The woman who had answered the phone at the neurology clinic in Sioux Falls was as movable as a gigantic stone wall.

"The doctor does not take phone calls from people who are not patients." If possible, she sounded bored with the entire conversation.

Oh, for God's sake. That did it—no more Mr. Nice Lawyer. "Does he take calls from lawyers? Lawyers who have a detailed understanding of the Patients' Bill of Rights? Lawyers who know that a verdict for the defendant—that would be your boss—can cost just as much as settling out of court? Does Dr. Klein really want to see his malpractice insurance costs go through the roof? Because if he does, you can just keep giving me the runaround. I can always call back when I've got a subpoena and a news crew."

When the woman didn't have a pat comeback for that, Nick had to smile. Nothing like the threat of litigation to shut up the obstinate. Then he heard a click. Had she just hung up on him? Hell, no. He would sue them into the last century.

But before he could do anything, the gentle sound of Muzak filled his ear. Ah, that was more like it.

Tanya stuck her head in his office. "How's it going?"

"On hold." He winked at her, and was rewarded with a hint of a blush.

"You've got a meeting in fifteen minutes with Councilwoman Mankiller and Ms. Armstrong," she reminded him before winking back.

Nick craned his neck to watch her turn around and walk away. Sure, he was dog-tired. He'd been at Tanya's house until eight last night, then driven home and spent five hours researching the known health risks associated with fracking. That was a whole different reason why he had to keep Tanya in the dark about this. What he'd found—childhood cancers, strokes and more unexplained deaths than he could count—would scare the hell out of her. Honestly, it scared the hell out of him, too. He didn't want to burden her with the worst-case diagnoses. In this case, ignorance was truly bliss. He didn't want to worry her until he had confirmation and a plan of action.

"This is Dr. Klein," a deep voice crackled at the other

end of the phone. He sounded pissed, condescending and more than a little concerned.

Nick knew the type perfectly. No doubt, this doctor thought he was better than everyone else, but he lived in terror of being proven wrong.

"Dr. Klein, my name is Nicholas Long. I'm a junior partner with Sutcliffe, Watkins and Monroe, based in Chicago, and I'm representing the interests of the Red Creek Lakota Tribe in an ongoing matter." He paused for dramatic effect. "Do I have your attention yet, or will I need to tell you what I told your receptionist?"

Dr. Klein cleared his throat. "How can I help you today, Mr. Long?"

Oh, yeah—Nick knew the type. "Dr. Klein, I understand that you've turned away members of the Red Creek tribe because you do not honor South Dakota's CHIP program. Is that correct?"

After a strained pause, Dr. Klein said, "We have a limited number of resources available to us. Due to ongoing budgeting issues at the state level, certain segments of the population—"

Boy, it was amazing what one could blame on "budgeting issues," including denying care to sick children. "You won't work if you don't get paid—that's what you're really saying, correct?"

Another strained pause. "We all have bills to pay, Mr. Long."

That was a "yes." "Well, I'd like to make you an offer. I'm going to need a series of tests run on several members of the tribe. I'm going to need the results of those tests in days, not weeks, and I'm going to be paying for these tests in cash, up front." Eliminating the baggage of insurance should do the trick.

But it didn't. Nick could hardly believe his ears when

the man came back with, "I'd be happy to have the re-ceptionist schedule the next available appointment. I believe I have an opening in three months."

"Are you serious?" Because three months was liter-ally one-fourth of Bear's life. No way Nick was going to put his son's health on the back burner for months.

"Mr. Long, I'm sure you can appreciate that time is money."

The statement hung out there. Unbelievable, Nick thought. Dr. Klein was trying to shake him down. Clearly, this man did not know with whom he was deal-ing. Nick took a deep breath and focused on keeping his cool. Shouting would betray his position. A calm, level approach would be that much more menacing. "I'll make you a deal, Dr. Klein. You give me your earliest appointment—as in this week—and I won't report you to the authorities. I'm sure they might buy that weak 'budgeting issues' argument, but combining a denial of care with soliciting bribes? You might get to keep your license, Dr. Klein, but I can promise you a long, expensive investigation. Would you care to contemplate your finances after you pay your lawyer, malpractice insurance premiums and the time away from paying clients, or would you rather just give me a damn ap-pointment now?"

The silence went on for a beat too long. Nick was either about to win this little battle or he was about to be hung up on.

Then Dr. Klein cleared his throat. "I, uh, could have an opening this Thursday." His voice was quiet and un-deniably nervous.

Nick smiled. Victory, no matter how small the battle, was always sweet. "I'd like to take that appointment, Dr. Klein. I'm also sure that any related tests—a complete blood count, metabolic panel, heavy metal, CT scans or MRIs—will be completed immediately." How much was this doctor going to charge him for this? It didn't matter. Bear's health was worth it.

"I think we're on the same page, then." The condescending tone was back in force, which made Nick think that someone else had walked into the room.

"So glad to hear it." As long as that page was that Dr. Klein was an A-number-one jerk. Greedy men shouldn't be in charge of other people's lives.

Dr. Klein's voice got muffled, as if he was holding the receiver against his chest, but Nick thought he heard the man telling someone to cancel his golf appointment.

Nick hung up and sat there, staring at his desk. Yes, he had the appointment, which was something. But Nick couldn't shake the feeling of pervasive dread that had built up over the past twenty-four hours.

No need to panic. He needed to stay focused on his case, that was all. His resolve set, he grabbed his boxed-up water samples and headed to the front desk. Tanya was typing something in a spreadsheet, her hair wound into a loose braid. More than anything, Nick wanted to sneak up behind her and plant a kiss on her neck. But that would be unprofessional on several different levels, so instead he made sure to keep the desk between the two of them. "We're going Thursday morning."

"Really?" Her face lit up, like she'd just unwrapped diamonds on Christmas morning. "How?"

"I can be very persuasive when the situation calls for it." So he wasn't touching her. He couldn't stop himself from giving her the kind of smile that any idiot would be able to guess the meaning of. "It's at nine-fifteen, so we'll have to leave your house by seven-thirty."

Tanya leaned forward, her eyes fastened on him. "You want to spend the night?"

Yes was the short answer, but... "I have to see how much work I get done before that. I'll drive us all, though, okay?" He heard the front door open behind him. Right—this was not the time or place to be making sleeping arrangements. "Oh, and make sure this goes out today." He handed her the package with his water samples in it. "Overnight."

Tanya's face was bright red. "Yes, Mr. Longhair. Good morning, Ms. Armstrong."

Nick turned to see Rosebud shaking her head at the both of them. "Good morning, Tanya. Heard you put in quite the appearance at the powwow this weekend, Nick."

Tanya only got redder. But at least she was still smiling. Much better than the last time the three of them had been standing here. "I just showed up and played with my son. Was that somehow scandalous?" He kept his tone full of innocent surprise.

Nick was glad Rosebud was on his side because the way she was staring at him was intense. "No, I suppose not. So is this common knowledge now or just an open secret?"

Nick glanced at Tanya, who looked deeply uncomfortable with this entire conversation. "Tanya and I have reached an understanding. I'm sure I don't care what anyone else thinks about a private matter."

"Boy," Rosebud said with an unlawyerly giggle, "you *have* been gone a long time." Even Tanya managed a weak smile at that.

The phone on the desk buzzed, and Tanya answered it, sounding very businesslike and not the least bit embarrassed. "Yes? Yes. I'll send them down." She hung up and tried to give Nick a stern glare. "Councilwoman Mankiller is waiting for you both."

"We mustn't keep Aunt Emily waiting," Rosebud said as she headed down the hall. Then she paused, causing Nick to nearly trip over her. "And Tanya? I'm glad things are going well."

"Me, too," Nick heard her say. *Me, too,* he mentally agreed as he swung past his office to grab his notes.

Once he was settled into his seat at the conference table, the door safely shut, Emily Mankiller asked him, "So, where does our case stand?"

Time to get down to business. While he was sure that both Emily and Rosebud were happy that he'd come back and reconnected with Tanya and Bear, the fact of the matter was that he'd been hired to do a job, and now was the time to do it. "The first water sample from inside the contaminated zone is headed to the lab today, and on Thursday, I'll be accompanying a tribal member to the leading neurologist in the state for the first round of testing for heavy metals and other contaminants. If Rosebud's theory that the fracking polluted the groundwater of the Dakota River and a ten-mile radius is correct, then both the water and the people who are drinking it will test positive. Once we have confirmed the results through independent testing and lined up experts who will be able to testify about what the results mean, we'll have Midwest Energy…" *by the balls* was what he almost said, because that was the language used in Chicago. But this wasn't Chicago, and he didn't think Emily, or even Rosebud, would appreciate such imagery. "We'll have them on the ropes."

Both women exchanged a look that Nick interpreted as "we hired the right man for the job." Which was a huge compliment. "Impressive," Rosebud said. "Who are you taking to the neurologist?"

Nick paused, wishing he had a glass of water. Suddenly, all those horrifying diagnoses and death statistics were standing out in 3-D in his mind's eye. Must be the late night after the early morning, he thought. He couldn't afford to come apart at the seams—not now, and as sure as hell not in the courtroom later. "My son."

The silence that came over the room was downright painful. Before either woman could offer him weak reassurances, Nick went on, "The second person I'm going to have tested is Doreen Rattling Blanket."

"Who's going to pay for the tests?" Rosebud's voice was low but serious. Very serious.

"I am, at least for my immediate family. That includes water treatment. The tribe may have to look into trucking in fresh water for families who have been contaminated. Those costs would be recouped with a judgment in our favor." Emily nodded in approval. "What I'd like from you two is a list of other people who have developed unusual health issues since the alleged fracking took place. Bear doesn't speak. Doreen acts like she's suffered several strokes and her weight gain is unusual, too. Within that ten-mile radius, who else is sick? I'll pay the up-front cost for all the testing on the assumption that those costs will be reimbursed by the judgment against Midwest Energy. But I need more than just two people. I need dozens."

Emily Mankiller cleared her throat. "Tanya would know who's not well. She's my eyes on the rez. But she doesn't know anything about this case, does she?"

"I'm maintaining all appropriate confidentiality," he assured her, knowing that he shouldn't be irked by the suggestion that he'd tell Tanya everything but annoyed all the same. "She will be going to the doctor's visit with me and Bear, obviously. I will not discuss this case with her without your express permission. But someone's going to have to tell her something if she's going to be doing oral interviews on people's health."

Emily nodded. "I don't see a conflict here. She's got a right to know. You have our permission to discuss the situation with her, but I would recommend you not go in with guns blazing. There's no need to spark a panic."

Nick looked at her, but the older woman didn't even blink. That was a pretty slick way of telling him to wait until he had some proof—and walked a damn fine line between forthcoming and withholding. Unfortunately, Emily had a point. Right now, he was guessing. It was an educated guess, to be sure, but he had no proof that Bear's silence had a thing to do with the fracking. If he sprung this on Tanya now, at the very least, she'd lose a lot of sleep over it, and at the worst, she'd panic. And panic was one of those things that spread like wildfire—once it was out there, it was impossible to control. "Agreed."

"All we ask is that you use your best judgment on when and how you communicate about the case with Tanya," Rosebud added, striking a warmer tone. "How you do that is completely up to your discretion."

Emily nodded, looking tired. "We've fought for our land for so long…" She looked at Rosebud, who covered her aunt's hand with her own. "I never thought we'd be poisoned by it." She seemed worn down by the fight, but that exhaustion didn't last long. She glanced up, and Nick saw that she wasn't giving up anytime soon. "We can win this, Nick. We have to. I know that Tanya will be one hundred percent behind us. I'll talk to her about doing oral interviews, but I think it's best to hold off on that assignment until the situation with Bear has been resolved. In the meantime, you'll keep us apprised of the test results?"

"Absolutely." He cleared his throat. What he wouldn't give for some water—clean water. "Depending on the results, though, I may have to be absent from the office. I want to assure you both personally that if that worst-case scenario happens, I will keep working on the job that I was hired to do."

The silence that followed was even more uncomfortable. Finally, Rosebud said, "You'll tell us if you reach the point where you have to recuse yourself, won't you?"

"Absolutely." But more than ever, he didn't trust this case in some outsider's hands. Would Jenkins, back in Chicago, give a damn about a little boy who couldn't speak? Would he front the money for expensive tests for ten to fifteen percent of the tribe's population? Would he do everything—*everything*—in his power to bring Midwest Energy to justice? Or would Jenkins punt the ball and take the first piddly settlement Midwest offered just to be done with the whole thing?

Nick knew the answer. And he knew what he had to do.

Ten

"Just hold him steady," a small woman with a large needle said.

Tanya squeezed her eyes shut. She had Bear on her lap. Nick held Bear's arm down against the table. He stood between them and the nurse, shielding Bear's face from that needle. "Bear? Look at Daddy, honey. Hi!" Nick was saying, and even with her eyes shut, Tanya could hear him making funny faces.

She couldn't look, though. Even though this blood draw was for Bear, just the thought of her baby hurting made her nauseous. Of course, if she was going to throw up and pass out, where better than in a hospital?

Then Bear's body went stiff and he slammed his head back into Tanya's chin. "Shh, shh," she whispered in his ear. Again, it was pointless, but it was all she could do without crying.

"I know," Nick was saying, his voice kind. "Almost done—oh, you're being such a good boy! Yes, you are!"

Despite the upsetting situation, Tanya smiled at Nick. He acted as if he had this whole fatherhood thing down cold.

That was almost as important as how he didn't act. At no point in the past four days had he acted like she owed him. Last night, dinner had been as normal as possible, considering Nick was at her place and spent the night. After she'd cleared the dishes, he'd pulled out a fancy-looking laptop and done some work before he'd read Bear his bedtime story. Then they'd made love on the couch again. It was the sort of night that Tanya desperately wanted to get used to.

She could do without the blood draws, however, even though she knew it was for the best. How long was this lady going to keep taking blood?

The whole time, Tanya's mind spun. The doctor spent a large part of their appointment talking about how quickly kids bounced back from stuff like "aphonia"—which was the big, fancy word he'd used for ten minutes before Tanya had figured out he was talking about Bear's silence. The doctor had said he was going to run some standard tests to nail down the exact cause of the aphonia, but "We might need to investigate some environmental causes," in his professional opinion. *Environmental*—that was the word that kept Tanya's brain whirling.

Whatever the cause was, the doctor had been clear—Bear could recover easily from the aphonia once the cause was identified. For the first time in months, Tanya wasn't resigned to Bear being disabled. Instead, she was hopeful that he could be fixed. And it was all thanks to Nick.

Finally, the needle part was over. The nurse left the IV port in, so Bear wouldn't have to have another stick at the hospital. She wrapped it up so Bear wouldn't pull at it, then stuck a Curious George bandage on the top. Tanya looked at the huge cluster of vials full of Bear's blood and felt more than a little ill. What a strange feeling, she thought. Blood had never bothered her before, but something about this situation made her extra uneasy. Tests meant results, and while the doctor had glossed over the really bad stuff, results could mean some very scary diseases. Tanya felt as if she'd spent too long ignoring a small leak and suddenly it had become a flood that she couldn't manage by herself.

"Now, you're heading over to the hospital for a CT scan, correct?" The nurse briskly removed her gloves and sat down at her computer. "Do you know where you're going?"

"Yes," Nick said, and Tanya fell in love with him all over again. He was here; he was strong; he was in complete control of this situation. She wasn't struggling to do all of this alone. She felt as if the weight of the world had been, well, not lifted, but shared. And for that, she was grateful.

They walked down a hallway and past the open door to what looked like the doctor's personal office. Tanya had formed an opinion of the man from the way his receptionist had answered the phone, but in person, he was friendly—almost eager to see that Bear got any possible test he needed. Like right now. "How did it go?" he asked, popping up from his desk.

Nick answered for her. "Fine."

The two men seemed to be staring each other down. If anything, Nick looked like he was close to threatening Dr. Klein. What was that all about? The awkwardness of the moment had Tanya wondering what, exactly, Nick had done to get this appointment.

"People don't ignore you when you're rich, and they don't write you off when you're powerful," he'd said. Clearly, he knew what he was talking about.

"We look forward to hearing from you as soon as the results are in," Nick said, and there was no mistaking the directive in his tone.

"I'll be in touch." And there was no mistaking the doctor's begrudging reply.

Must have been a heck of a phone call, Tanya thought with a smile. How nice that, for once, things had gone in her favor. She had Nick to thank for that, too.

"Ready?" Nick asked as he took Bear from her. Thumb in his mouth, Bear snuggled his head onto Nick's shoulder, then sneaked his other hand up and grabbed on to Nick's hair. Nick responded by leaning down and kissing Bear on the forehead, then reaching his hand out to her. She laced her fingers with his and they walked out to the truck, where Nick buckled Bear into the correctly installed car seat.

This was happiness, she decided as she took her place next to Nick. The only way things could have possibly been better was if they weren't traveling between a doctor's office and a hospital. But she felt sure that with Nick sharing the load, it wouldn't be long before they figured out what was wrong with Bear and had it fixed. It wouldn't be the worst case. Bear was going to be fine. She just knew it.

As a computer voice in Nick's phone told them where to turn, Tanya found herself daydreaming about what might happen after that. Nick was keeping his promise, being the father she'd hoped he would be. He helped wash the dinner dishes and tucked Bear in—promising that he'd get his very own bed really soon—and just kept being wonderful. That's what it was. Wonderful.

But, greedy as she was, she wanted more than just a sharing of the parenting load. Sex between them was… well, she flushed just thinking about the way Nick had made her come and then come again last night on the couch. Sex was *better* now than it had ever been before, but instead of scratching her Nick-sized itch, she only wanted to scratch it some more. She didn't want to just have dinner with him twice a week. She wanted to have dinner with him every day. She didn't want to share just a couch with him. She wanted to share her bed. Heck, she wanted to share her life.

Tanya wanted to be married to Nick, which was different than what she'd always wanted before. Back when she'd been a crazy-in-love girl, she'd wanted to *get* married. She'd dreamed of how Nick would propose and what her wedding dress would look like—same for the cake and the whole ceremony—the whole nine yards of a wedding. She realized now that all those years ago, she'd put very little thought into actually living her life with Nick. Now, though, she hadn't spent a single moment on any of that stuff. A wedding ceremony was just that—a ceremony. She wanted more than that. Was it wrong to want a nice house? Was it wrong to want another baby—maybe two—with Nick?

She wanted a life with him. She wanted to be a wife to his husband. She wanted to be a family.

The question she couldn't answer was whether or not she would get that. In the back of her mind, she couldn't shake the feeling that Nick would get tired—of her, of being a daddy, of the rez, of being an Indian again. The place he was renting was super-nice compared to Tanya's run-down little house—but the way he talked about his *real* home in Chicago made it pretty clear that he couldn't wait to get back to the city.

Bear, she felt, was what was really holding Nick here. He was genuinely concerned about the boy's health. Yes, that only made Tanya love him more, but underneath that, she sensed a judgment. Did he blame her? Hell, she already blamed herself for not getting Bear to the doctor earlier. She'd *tried,* she really had, but she didn't have the pull or the power Nick did.

Did he see it like that? Or did he think that she hadn't tried hard enough? She just couldn't shake the feeling that not only was she not good enough to hold Nick, but also that deep down, he didn't think she was a good enough mother. Even if Bear was fine or if this not-speaking thing of his was a quick and easy fix, Tanya couldn't get past the fact that other people would hold it against her. She was the boy's mother, for heaven's sake. She should have been the one demanding—and getting—appointments. To anyone on the outside, she would seem like a horrible mother—oblivious at best but neglectful at the very least.

She didn't want anyone to think she didn't love her son. Least of all Nick.

She needed to get a grip. Nick wasn't holding anything over her head. He'd made no comments, no insinuations that he held her responsible for this. And actually, there was a small chance that she wasn't. What had that doctor meant by "environmental"?

"Babe?"

Tanya snapped to attention. "Huh?"

Nick shot her a sideways smile as he turned into a huge parking garage. "We're here. Penny for your thoughts."

She was being silly. She had to keep a hold of the reality of the situation, and the reality was, Nick had been back on her couch for only five days. He was doing a fine job of proving his honorable intentions so far, but five days wasn't long enough to base any major decisions on. She needed to stay focused on the present, not some dreamy future that may or may not come to pass, and the immediate future was a CT scan. The doctor had made it sound like a routine test, nothing to be afraid of. She needed to make sure she focused on getting Bear better. Everything else could be dealt with later.

"I was just thinking how glad I am that you're here." That was the unvarnished truth. She wasn't sure she'd have made it through the blood draw without him, and they hadn't even gotten to the CT scan yet. Dr. Klein had said that Bear would be sedated. She had no idea how she would have handled that without Nick to be her pillar of strength.

"Yeah?" He parked in an open space on the second level. "A fun family day out at the hospital, huh?"

Tanya glanced over her shoulder. Bear, no doubt already tired out from the poking and prodding, had fallen asleep. He seemed so peaceful—innocence embodied. "It's just that..." Her throat closed up. So many emotions—guilt and worry and things she couldn't even name—flooded her. She just wanted things to be okay. "I wish I knew how this had happened. The doctor said it might be environmental." Frustrated tears clogged up her throat. "I didn't feed him tainted food or anything. How could it be environmental? I mean, it's not like I made his formula with gasoline," she went on. "But I think you're right—Mom's sick, too. Do you think it's something in the water?"

The moment she said it out loud, she heard an audible click in her head. Of course it was the water—how could she have not seen it before? "Nick—it's the water! The water at Mom's house—it has to be! Bear's there all day, five days a week! Why else would they be sick when I'm not?"

Again, she didn't know what she expected him to do, but he didn't do it. Moving slowly, he turned the truck off, then sat there for a few moments, his hands on the wheel. "Tanya," he said, and she heard nothing but business and danger in his voice. "Do you know what fracking is?"

"No." Was she supposed to? "Other than it's got something to do with your case."

He took a deep breath, and for the life of her, Tanya thought that this must be what he looked like when he was arguing in court. "Fracking is short for hydraulic fracturing. It's where a mixture of chemicals is injected into the ground and exploded, basically, to release the natural gas stored under the bedrock."

Tanya's chest felt like it had caved in. Breathing was almost impossible. "What are you saying?"

"You're right—I think it's the water. I think the water was contaminated when Midwest Energy Company drilled under the Dakota River and fracked to get the natural gas located under the rez. The reason the Red Creek Lakota hired me is to prove that when Midwest did that, they contaminated the groundwater and the Dakota River." Finally, he did look at her. Even though he sounded like a lawyer, he looked like he was worried—about her. "My job is to prove that Bear's silence, your mother's headaches—all of that is connected to the contamination."

"You—you knew this?" Confusion gave way to a blinding rage that coursed through her body. "You already knew this—and you didn't tell me?" She fumbled for the door handle without really thinking. She had to get out of here, but then she remembered that if she bailed, she'd be bailing on Bear, too. Damn it.

"I don't *know* anything—nothing that can be proven," he hurried to add, reaching for her. She shrank back in horror. "It's just a guess. I was going to wait to talk to you about this until after I had the test results from today—those will tell us if I'm right or if I'm wrong. It could be something else." His voice changed from the all-business tone to one that was decidedly more pleading. "I was going to tell you, but I didn't want to worry you with a worst-case scenario without proof. I could still be wrong. I wanted to make sure I was right." He looked over his shoulder at his son. "I don't want to be, Tanya. I want to be wrong. I don't want you to worry. That's all."

"What if you're right? This is for your case, Nick!" Her voice had gotten louder because Nick winced and checked on Bear again. "This is your case," she repeated in a whisper. "What does that mean for me? For us?" She had seen some of those lawyer shows. She was pretty sure that lawyers couldn't sleep with their clients. Would he pick his big case over her?

Then another, bigger fear smacked her upside the head. "You're going to use Bear as evidence *and*…" The *and* there was huge. And she was going to have to testify. Bear couldn't talk. She would have to do it for him.

She'd have to be on the stand. Which meant the Midwest Energy lawyers—because she knew anything with the name Midwest Energy had to have lawyers, lots of them—would cross-examine her.

They would make sure everyone knew she was a terrible mother.

"You cannot use our son as evidence." Because if

Bear wasn't evidence, Tanya wouldn't have to testify. "You leave him out of this."

He looked like she'd stabbed him in the shoulder with a plastic fork. He was the one who'd been holding out on her. He had no right to look so wounded.

"Tanya, I have to. This case is important—not just for me," he added sharply. "It's important for the tribe. For the land—your land. I have to use Bear's records as evidence."

Oh, he was going to pull the whole this-land-is-your-land crap? To hell with that. "No, you don't. If it's the water, there's got to be other people you can use. Not me. Not Bear."

He sighed, a sound that was patience teetering on the edge of a high ledge. "Emily Mankiller was going to talk to you about that—after we got this thing with Bear squared away. You're right. It's not just your mom and Bear. We were going to ask you to compile a list of other people with unusual symptoms that could be traced back to the contamination. She said you're the best person to do it, and I believe her."

The compliment helped. She shouldn't let herself be swayed by simple flattery, but hey, when the boss said nice things, it never hurt. She took a deep breath, trying to force some of the air back into her lungs. "Sure. Great. Just don't use Bear, Nick. I…I couldn't handle it. Mom will do it." She hoped. But it was one thing for a grown woman who had been feeling bad to testify under oath that she hadn't been able to afford medical care. It was quite another to be the woman who hadn't gotten her kid to the doctor. "Don't make me." That last bit came out sounding more scared than she wanted it to.

He looked at her—not the worried father, not the man who'd held her close just last night. No, Nick Longhair the lawyer looked at her long and hard. Something cold flickered in his eyes, and it made Tanya feel trapped in the truck. But then it softened. "You'll find me more cases I can tie to the pollution?"

Anything to keep from having her reputation smeared for the rest of her life. "Absolutely."

Nick slipped his hand around the back of her neck and pulled her in close. "You focus on Bear for now." He kissed her then. She leaned into him, feeling his strong chest, his equally strong arms. He wasn't just here—he was here for *her*.

For the first time, he was here when she needed him. With him by her side, she could face blood draws and CT scans. As long as he was with her, she could face whatever diagnosis all these tests pointed to.

As long as he was here. She just had no idea how long that would be.

By the time the CT scan was finished, it was almost four. While they waited for someone to come get them, Nick called Councilwoman Mankiller to explain that neither he nor Tanya would be back in the office today. Then, as Tanya listened in a state of shock, Nick told *her* boss that she wouldn't be in tomorrow either.

As soon as he hung up or clicked off or whatever people did with those slick cell phones that didn't even have buttons, Tanya was all over him. "I'm *what* now?"

"You're not going to work tomorrow."

He said it in such a matter-of-fact way that Tanya had to wonder if she'd forgotten some conversation they'd had. "Is that so?"

He nodded. "I'm taking you both back to my place tonight."

"Is that *so*." First, he knew about pollution, now he

was calling her in sick. When had she lost control? More important, when had Nick decided to take it?

She glared at him. And the irritating thing was, it took him a moment to notice. "What?"

"I have a job. I have bills to pay." *I have my own life,* she wanted to add.

Then Nick did something even more irritating: he grinned at her. Sure, he looked a little tired—they'd been in this particular waiting room for several hours now—but he still managed to appear deeply amused. "And I swear to God, if you say, 'No one in Chicago talks like you,' I'm going to smack that smile right off your face."

He bit his lip. He was actively *almost* laughing at her. The most irritating thing of all was how good he looked doing it—not that Nick looked adorable, but if he did, this was it. "First off," he began when he appeared to have himself back under control, "you're going to be exhausted tomorrow."

"But—"

"Second," he went on, "Bear is going to come out of anesthesia at any moment, and he's probably going to be a wreck."

"Yeah, but—"

"Because," he cut her off again, "he's probably going to be dealing with the anesthesia effects for a day or so, and I don't think your mother is capable of handling him if she's not feeling well."

"Well—"

"And we'd already agreed that you were going to spend the weekend with me, so this makes the most sense. I have a couple of movies I picked out for Bear to watch. I thought he'd like *Dumbo.*"

"You do? You did?" That had always been something

she'd dreamed of having—a TV. Some days, a girl just wanted to curl up on the couch and watch a cartoon. "But I didn't pack anything…"

"I grabbed a few things for you when you were buckling Bear in. And I have plenty of stuff for Bear at my place. I'll leave you the truck in case you need to pick up anything."

Tanya was pretty sure a high-powered lawyer had just talked circles around her because she was awfully damn dizzy. "And you were going to tell me all this… when?"

He opened his mouth, ready with the smooth reply, but at that moment, a nurse came through the doors and called their names.

"Babies are often upset when the sedation wears off. This is a normal reaction," was all Tanya heard before she saw her son in the arms of another nurse. His mouth was open, tears streaming down his face, his body rigid.

Normal? Whatever argument she'd been losing with Nick was forgotten as they rushed to their son. Tanya didn't care where she slept or if her clothes were the same ones she'd had on yesterday or how many circles Nick could talk around her. All she cared about was doing whatever she could to make sure her baby was okay.

In his own domineering way, she was pretty sure that was what Nick cared about, too.

Eleven

"This way," Nick said as he led Tanya up the stairs. He turned on the hall light and waited for her to catch up. Bear was fast asleep in her arms, and she looked exhausted.

Hell, he was beat. More than beat. He hadn't expected how hard it would be for him to keep some sort of professional objectivity toward today's procedures. In theory, he needed to keep his case near the forefront of his mind. But when faced with the reality of a baby having a "normal" reaction to drugs and a mother who broke down in tears because she couldn't calm that baby down—well, anyone human would have to admit that today had been a highly personal kind of day.

"This is Bear's room." He turned on the bedside lamp instead of the ceiling light so he wouldn't wake the boy up.

"Oh...um..." Tanya blinked in what was essentially wordless shock. "A car?"

Nick gave her a tired smile. The bed had come in a few days ago. He'd gone with the race-car bed because it had higher sides—all the better to keep the little tyke from rolling out, the salesman had said. But yeah, he probably should have warned Tanya about the Corvette with a mattress in the middle. "It was on sale," he offered, hoping that would help. He pulled the sheet back and waited for Tanya to lay Bear down.

She didn't. Instead, she looked like she was hugging Bear extra-hard. "Tanya?"

"It's just…he was so upset today, and—and—" Her voice broke on the end.

It hurt a part of Nick that he hadn't even realized existed. "And?"

"And he's never slept by himself before. He's never been apart from me." She said this last like she was ashamed of it. Like Nick would be ashamed of her for it. "What if he wakes up because of the drugs and stuff from today? What if he has another bad reaction and he needs me and I'm not here for him? I'm not a bad mother."

What? Who was accusing her of being a bad mom? But before Nick could make any sense of that last statement, she turned a teary set of eyes to him. Then defiance flashed in them. "You said I could sleep wherever I wanted. I should stay in here with him. Just for tonight."

This was the sort of argument that was hard to lose and harder to win. He loved Bear, he really did. But he didn't want the boy in his bed. He wanted to keep that place special, just for him and Tanya. Luckily, Nick had an ace up his sleeve. Thank God for pushy salesmen, he thought. "He'll be fine, babe. The doctor said he'd sleep it off, remember?"

"But what if—"

"I have a video monitor. See?" He turned on the small camera next to the lamp. "The screen is next to my bed. You can roll over and see him anytime."

"Really?" She didn't say it like she didn't believe him; she said it like she'd never even heard of a video monitor before.

"Really." He made sure to keep his voice gentle. It was late, and they were all tired, and the last thing he wanted was to cross some nearly invisible line that would have her digging in her heels. "Here." He held out his arms to her, and after another squeeze, she handed Bear off to him.

Nick did a better job of laying his son down this time. Bear's eyes fluttered, then he rolled over and stuck his thumb in his mouth. "See?" Nick whispered as he flipped off the light. "He'll be fine."

Tanya nodded, but she didn't look like she entirely believed him. However, she let him take her hand and lead her out of the room and across the hall to the master suite. "The bathroom is over there, and it's got all the things you'll need," he said as he handed her the bag of her clothes he'd grabbed.

She looked at him and blinked a couple of times. She looked like she was already asleep except she didn't know it yet. "Nick."

"Yeah?"

"I'm going to let this ride right now, but later, we're going to have a discussion about what and when you tell me stuff, like pollution that might be hurting our son and packing my clothes for an overnight visit without my knowledge."

An unfamiliar tinge of guilt washed over him. Not so much for springing the overnight stay—well, maybe just a little—but because when they did have that "discussion," he knew he'd agree to make all decisions *with* her instead of *for* her, and he knew that if Bear's tests were positive, he'd still need him as his first, best piece of evidence. Juries loved kids, especially kids as cute and innocent as Bear.

Nick was sure that given time to get used to the idea, Tanya would come around to understanding how important this would be for the tribe. That was the Tanya he knew—the one who fought for their people's land, the one who refused to leave it. She'd just had a bad day—they all had. In the morning, or in a few days, she'd see his side.

But he wouldn't convince her tonight. So he changed the subject. "There's the monitor. I'll turn it on."

Tanya sighed a little too loudly, but true to her word, she let it ride.

They took turns in the bathroom, then climbed into bed. It was only 9:15 p.m., but it felt like it was three in the morning. As far as he could remember, this was the first time he'd slept all night in a bed with Tanya. For some reason, he felt sentimental as he pulled her back into his arms. She lay on her side, watching the monitor that was less than a foot from the bed.

He expected to fall asleep in seconds, but he didn't. Her back and bottom were warm against his front, and with every breath, her chest rose under his hands. It wasn't a sexual kind of touching, but something more. He knew she'd be here all weekend, but still, he wanted to hold on to this moment of intimacy.

Her breathing had been regular for some time—five, maybe ten minutes—and he thought she'd nodded off. Bear hadn't moved on the monitor either. The house felt asleep. But then she asked, "Nick?"

"Yeah?"

She was quiet for a moment, but then she said, "I've been thinking about something you said—that you didn't bail on me."

Was this going to turn into another push back? Nick swallowed, trying to figure out the best way to reply, but she went on. "I don't think that—not that exactly."

"What did you think?"

"I thought…" Her voice was so quiet that he had to lean forward to catch the rest of her words. "I thought I wasn't enough for you. I wasn't enough to make you want to stay."

"No." That word flew out of his mouth so fast that she jumped in his arms. He forced himself to take a deep breath. This wasn't an argument. She was being honest. The least he could do was return the favor. He tightened his grip on her. "That's not why I left."

She laced her fingers with his. "Then why? Why did you go, and why didn't you come back? I waited for you."

Thirteen years of waiting. Thirteen years of thinking that she wasn't good enough for him, when it had always been the other way around.

He leaned forward and kissed her neck. "You know why I never asked you to come visit me when I went off to college?"

"No." He could hear the hurt in her voice. It was faint, but still there after all these years.

Damn it, he'd messed up so badly. He had to marvel that she still managed to love him. "I lived in my car."

She let out a little gasp. "What?"

"I was homeless. It wasn't all bad," he hurried to add. "I mean, I spent a lot of time in the library—that's why I got such good grades. I showered at the gym. I crashed on a lot of couches. But I didn't have my own place. I lived out of my car."

In some respects, it had been humiliation on top of humiliation. Like the time the library janitor had called the campus police after finding him sleeping on a couch he'd pulled back behind a stack, or the time the local cops had arrested him for loitering when he'd parked in the Super Mart lot to sleep for one night. He couldn't have let Tanya see him living like that.

But the thing was, no matter how humiliating it had been, he'd always been warmer and cleaner and better fed than he had been living with his mother growing up. Even living in his car had been a drastic improvement over living in the burned-out camper with cardboard for windows.

"I had no idea." She sounded like she might start crying.

"No one did." No way in hell he would go around announcing his craptacular living arrangements. But he didn't want her to be upset. "It got better when I went to law school—I got some grants for being a minority, so I had enough cash for an apartment. But not a good one, you know? I wound up finding this guy who seemed just as poor as I was—a true starving artist. We shared this studio apartment, one couch on each side of the wall."

It had been a hellhole, no other word for it. Half a dozen locks on the door, cockroaches in the sink. It hadn't been exactly warm in the winter, but warm enough. The plumbing functioned and the stove worked.

"Seemed?"

"Yeah. Arthur the artist. We weren't so much friends as cohorts in suffering. He wanted to be a painter, so he spent all his money on supplies."

"Seemed," she said again, more to herself than to

him. "So, I guess that's my other question—how did you go from sleeping on a couch to being this huge lawyer? I mean, I'm not saying you didn't earn it, and I'm not saying I didn't think you couldn't do it, but I never understood how it actually happened. No one on the rez knows. You just became this big shot, like by magic."

He smiled, even though she couldn't see it. "It felt a little bit like magic—I was in the right place at the right time. What happened was, my second year of law school, Arthur the artist told me he had to go to this family party. He made it sound like it was going to be this hugely boring thing, but he said, 'There'll be a ton of food, if you want to come.' And I wasn't about to pass up a free meal."

"So you went."

"I did. And it turned out that Arthur the artist was Arthur Sutcliffe, nephew of Marcus Sutcliffe, of Sutcliffe, Watkins and Monroe, and the 'family party' was a huge corporate event being held at the Art Institute of Chicago."

Nick still remembered the shock of walking in. He'd lived in Chicago for a year and a half, and hadn't made it to that part of town. Women in ball gowns and diamonds had swirled past him, champagne glasses in hand, on their way to kiss Arthur on the cheek and scold him for being late and looking like a slob. Nick had felt horribly out of place in his best clothes—a pair of unstained jeans, cowboy boots and a button-up flannel shirt. People had stared at him, that he knew, but he'd been too busy staring right back at men in tuxedos and priceless paintings—and the food. Tables twenty feet long with shrimp and caviar and more cookies and cakes than he'd ever seen at one time.

In that stunned moment, Nick had seen the future he

wanted. The jewels, the clothes, the food, the art—he'd walked into the perfect life. No one else in the room—with the exception of Arthur the starving artist—went to bed hungry or cold. No one else in the room worried about paying the electricity bill or whether the water was safe to drink. No one else at that party had ever lived in their car. Right then, Nick knew he could never go back to being poor and invisible. He was going to be somebody, and the somebody he was going to be was one of the somebodies in that room.

"You crashed a party and got a job?" Again, she sounded like she didn't believe it.

He had to agree that it was pretty unbelievable. "Marcus was pissed that Arthur had brought me, but Arthur told him I was in law school and an Indian." Which had been completely pointless. Nick still had his ponytail, and that, combined with his brown skin and last name, made that whole "is he or isn't he?" guessing game redundant. "I think—no, I know—that Marcus needed someone of color on staff. And when I turned out to be a good lawyer, well, so much the better."

The part that Nick skipped over was the part that came right before that. Rissa, Arthur's cousin, had introduced herself first. She'd been throwing off all sorts of interested signals to Nick, and she'd been the one who had introduced her father to Nick. Yes, Arthur had let him crash the party, but he'd gotten a job because the boss's daughter thought he'd been tall, dark and mysterious, and she wanted to keep him around.

Laying here with Tanya in his arms, Nick had a hard time remembering what it had been that he'd found so attractive about Rissa. She was beautiful, true, but looking back, it felt like a superficial kind of beauty. She had never made Nick feel like Tanya did right now, without even trying. Laying here with her, sharing his darkest secrets—Rissa would have made this entire exchange of information feel like a dangerous activity. With Tanya, it was different. Like instead of leaving him in a position of weakness, it only made him stronger.

She rolled over in his arms. Her face was less than three inches from his. He could kiss her, but that felt like a cheap way out. "He gave me an internship during my last year of law school because I'm a minority, but I earned the job offer." At least, he'd always believed that, until Marcus had ordered him to take the case of "those people." Now, he wasn't so sure. "When I got the job—and the salary that went with it—that's when I asked you to come with me. Things had changed. I could afford a nice place, and I could give you everything we'd always dreamed about."

And you said no. He didn't say the words out loud. He didn't have to. He could see them reflected in her face, the dull light of the video monitor making her look even sadder.

Maybe that had been why he'd taken up with Rissa. She was a woman who appreciated the value of things after all. She knew exactly what Nicholas Long could give her.

"You had it so much better than I did, you know. Your mom loved you—still does—and she had a nice house and she took care of you." All things he'd envied growing up. All things he swore his own son wouldn't do without. "I had to have something to offer you, something besides good grades, and living in a car wasn't it. You deserved better, Tanya, and I worked so hard to give it to you." He blinked, trying to get his vision to clear. Somehow, it had gotten blurry. "When you stayed behind, I thought you didn't believe I could do that. I thought you didn't believe in me."

And I wasn't coming back until I could prove you wrong. He didn't have to say that either. She knew.

Tanya touched her palm to his cheek, then she leaned in and placed her warm mouth on his ear. "I never doubted you, Nick. Not for a second."

This time, he did kiss her. None of those missed signals and mixed messages counted anymore. The past was done and gone, and good riddance. Today was what they had now, and God willing, tomorrow, too.

He had all these grand plans of making love to her on the big bed he'd bought just for them—long, slow sex where he got to devour her and her new curves— but it wasn't meant to be. Not tonight anyway. She dug her fingers into his back, his name whispered on her lips as their bodies moved together.

He'd had it all wrong. Somewhere along the way, he'd gotten it into his head that loving Tanya was an all-or-nothing proposition, and see what that had gotten him? Years of missing this—of missing her.

He'd let his pride, of all the stupid things, come between them. Only a fool would let that happen again. Nick liked to think he wasn't a fool. He wanted to take her with him.

But he knew, deep down, that she'd still balk at leaving. Despite the pollution and the poverty, he'd seen the look on her face when he'd repeated Emily Mankiller's high praise. Working for her tribe was what she'd always wanted to do. She was making a difference, damn it. She wouldn't bail now. If anything, she'd have renewed resolve to stay and fight for her land.

She'd want him to stay and fight with her.

Would he really give up everything—the condo, the job, the money—to come back to the rez?

Her body tightened around his, spurring him on. He pushed the unknowns out of his mind and concentrated on the woman.

Tanya.

Twelve

Nick hadn't wanted to go to work Friday. Bear had woken up at five, fussy and clingy, and Tanya had seemed worn out before the day had even begun. He'd thought about calling in and spending the day on the couch with the two of them watching cartoons and generally hanging out. But playing hooky wouldn't get him any closer to winning his case. So he'd packed up his bag, kissed Tanya goodbye and driven the hour to the office.

Once there, he was able to focus. He called Doreen and told her he was going to get her a doctor's appointment as soon as he could, and then he called a home improvement store and spent the extra cash on next-day installation for a water filtration system for her house. It wouldn't catch everything, but it was a start. Anything was an improvement.

He worked on the disclosure documents, too, putting

Bear at the top of his evidence list, and Dr. Klein behind him as a witness. He paused before adding Tanya to the list. Someone would have to speak for Bear after all. He hoped it wouldn't come to that. He hoped there was nothing wrong with his son. But he knew better. So he filled out the forms.

The morning had been moving along when the phone rang at exactly ten o'clock. Nick's stomach tightened. He couldn't say why, but something told him this was not good news. "Yes?"

"Mr. Long? Dr. Klein."

That feeling of unease grew. This early call seemed prompt—*too* prompt. Nick managed to swallow. His world seemed to shrink until it was a pinpoint black hole. "Yes, Dr. Klein. Do you have some information for me?"

"I have some results on your son, Edward Rattling Blanket. His bloodwork showed unusually high levels of xylene—actually, any level of that is unusual—and calcium." The doctor paused. The silence was horrifying. "Which, combined with the small, dark mass the CT showed on the baby's nape, indicates that he may have a tumor growing on his pituitary gland."

Darkness. That's all Nick saw. His son had cancer. And it had been caused by pollution.

He would grind Midwest Energy into the dust. By the time he got through with that company, nothing would remain. He would take them for everything they had and salt the earth behind him. If his son lived...

Nick swallowed again. It was all he could do to keep from screaming as he said, "What happens next?"

"I need an MRI to make sure the tumor isn't pressing against any blood vessels. It's uncommon, to say the least, to see a growth this size in a child this small.

Then we'll need to get him to a specialist in Minneapolis or—"

"Chicago," Nick said, his mouth operating on auto as his mind churned. Surgery. They were going to have to cut open his son.

"Chicago is fine. I've taken the liberty of setting up the MRI appointment for tomorrow at ten at the hospital. The boy will have to be sedated again. There's a chance the CT was misleading, but if it's not…things will happen very quickly."

Nick hung up. He had to tell Tanya. He could downplay the pollution aspect, but at this point, that seemed moot. Although he knew the *why* was incredibly important, it paled in comparison to the *how*—how they were going to make Bear better.

He was just about to pick up the phone when it rang again, startling him. "Hello?"

"Nicholas? This is Marcus. How's it going out there?"

The brakes in Nick's head slammed so hard that he swore he heard squealing. He shook his head, trying to get it back in the game. Marcus didn't know he had a son, and he probably didn't care one way or the other. The only thing Marcus cared about was winning. Was it possible that only a month ago, Nick had been the same way? "The case is going well. I've got some slam dunk evidence of Midwest Energy's malfeasance."

"Slam dunk, eh? What did you do—break into their headquarters?"

"No. I have people who have been drinking contaminated water with confirmed cases of cancer." At the edge of his thoughts was the possibility that he needed to recuse himself. He was way too close to this case now—it was personal on so many levels. But he wasn't going to, not now. Nick couldn't fathom what Jenkins would do about Bear, but he knew Jenkins wouldn't fight for Nick's son as hard as Nick would. No, he was in all the way.

Marcus had the decency to whistle in appreciation. "And you can tie it back to Midwest?"

"Absolutely." There was no room for doubt, not when the stakes were life and death. "I'm still collecting all the evidence, though." He had to get Doreen into the neurologist as soon as possible. What if she had cancer, too? The clock was ticking—for all of them. Then a new thought occurred to him. "Marcus, is your wife still on the board for Children's Memorial Hospital?"

"Of course. You know Gloria loves children. Why?"

"I need a neurologist—one who's as good in the operating room as he'll be on the witness stand. I have a confirmed case of brain cancer in a one-year-old child." *My son,* he wanted to add. But he didn't. He had to keep this professional. Objective. It felt like a betrayal. "I need the best of the best, someone who can go up and convince the jury that there's no way a baby could develop this cancer without being contaminated." Which was not untrue, but Nick wanted only the best doctor to operate on his son. "Juries love children, Marcus. I'm working on getting other people tested. This kid is just the tip of the iceberg, but he'll make our case for us."

"A one-year-old? Who'll testify for him?"

Nick kept his calm. He was a trained professional. He ignored the memory of Tanya's adamant arguments against using their son in this case and pressed on. "His mother, Tanya Rattling Blanket."

"Is she a reliable witness? You know how...*unreliable* some of those people can be."

Nick would keep his temper if it killed him—and at this rate, it might. Was this how Marcus talked about

Nick with other people? "She's not a drunk, if that's what you're implying. She's a very strong witness. College-educated, employed by the tribe. She'll be great on the stand." Once she knew she was going to be on the stand, that was.

But the moment he said it, he knew he'd slipped up, letting his defensiveness get the better of him. He could not afford to let Marcus and his "those peoples" throw him—what would that say about how Nick would handle himself in the courtroom? Nothing good, that much was certain.

Marcus paused. Nick swore he could hear the old man tapping his fingers on his desk. "You're not taking this case too personally, are you? We can't run the risk of letting one case give the firm a black eye if it's not handled properly. The firm's reputation must be protected at all costs."

The firm? What about the people? *His* people—they were the ones who needed protection. Nick bristled, but he kept it out of his voice. "Absolutely not. This is business—I know that. But no one needs to die to win this case."

"Of course. I'll have Gloria pull some strings. Does that mean you'll be back in town?"

Nick debated saying no. He didn't want to have to sit across from Marcus and wonder if the man saw a lawyer or an Indian. But Marcus was already questioning his ability to win this case, and Nick had to win. Not for the firm, though. For Bear. Which meant he had to play the game. "Yes. I want to make sure any potential evidence is collected properly. I need to document the surgery myself."

He needed to be there for Bear—and for Tanya. Damn it all, Marcus knew about Bear's diagnosis before Tanya did. That was backward. Everything felt inside out right now.

"I know Rissa has missed you. We'll do dinner while you're here."

"Sounds great." Which was a bald-faced lie. Right now, schmoozing and boozing it up with the extended Sutcliffe family seemed not only like a waste of his time, but a waste of his life.

He hung up and looked at the clock. 10:17 a.m. His whole world had changed in seventeen stinking minutes.

He took a few deep breaths and dialed the phone before the damn thing could ring again. "Hello, Tanya? I have something to tell you."

Thirteen

The last week had been a blur, much like the city lights outside the cab's windows. Yeah, Tanya knew Chicago was big, but the whole thing was so much *more* than she'd thought. Before she could make sense of the size, the cab Tanya, Nick and Bear were riding in pulled up in front of a fancy-looking building. A large black man in a hat and a blazer opened the door of the cab the moment the vehicle stopped moving. "Good evening, Mr. Long."

Okay, that was just weird. Did she know that Nick had dropped the "hair" from his name?

Heck, at this particular stage of things, she was lucky she still knew her own name. After all, any day that started with her getting on an airplane and flying to Chicago—all firsts for her—was pretty weird to begin with.

"Darius, these are my guests, Tanya and Bear Rattling Blanket. They have complete access to my home."

Nick held out his arms and took the sleeping Bear from Tanya.

"Pleasure to meet you, ma'am. Let me get those bags for you."

Tanya tried to smile, but the muscles around her mouth didn't seem to be moving. Nick lived in a place with a doorman. Was it wrong that she felt like she'd left reality behind the moment she'd gotten on a plane? "Hi."

Then she made the mistake of looking up. What looked like a solid wall of glass seemed to go on forever until it punctured the sky. That image made her want to laugh, but she managed to choke the errant giggle back. Holy cow, she couldn't even *see* the top of this building.

If she was making a fool of herself—and she was pretty sure she was—Darius gave no sign. The man was some kind of professional. "Did the things I ordered come in?"

"Yes, Mr. Long. All set up, as you requested."

Tanya didn't have any idea what they were talking about, but that was probably for the best. Then she was ushered into an elevator that was all shiny wood and shinier brass. The only other elevators she'd ever been in were crappy, beat-up ones that had gone up four floors in the university library. This—this was like the Mercedes of elevators. Then the doors closed and, after a brief pause, the elevator began silently zooming them up. And up. And up a whole bunch more.

She was tired, yes, and it had been a long day, but that didn't explain why she suddenly felt like giggling. This was patently ridiculous, she thought. Was this what Nick had been offering her four years ago? Doormen and classy elevators? And she'd turned him down...why?

Keep it together, she scolded herself. So what if it felt like she'd entered some sort of posh Twilight Zone, an alternate reality that she'd never thought really existed? She still had to be rational at least.

"Your ears may pop," Nick told her, the elevator still impossibly climbing.

This time, she did giggle. Nick shot her an odd look, which was even funnier. "You okay, Tanya?"

"Fine, fine." Which was patently untrue.

They were, quite literally, in rarified air. Her ears did, in fact, pop—and so did Bear's. He started squirming in Nick's arms. She had her arms halfway up to take the boy from Nick when he did the oddest thing—he lifted Bear up and blew a raspberry on his little baby tummy.

Bear's look of pain immediately changed into a goofy grin of pure delight. This time, Tanya didn't have to hold back her laugh. Nick blew another raspberry as the elevator doors opened. "This way," he said as he draped Bear over his shoulder like the boy was a sack of highly active potatoes. Tanya wasn't sure, but she thought he might be tickling Bear's feet—something that had the boy reeling off silent peals of joy.

They stepped out into a quiet hall that made Tanya feel like she had to stifle her voice again. The place had an odd feel to it, almost like the hushed reverence of a big church. Except this wasn't a sacred place. Unless one worshipped money.

Before she could think too much about that, Nick led them to one of only four doors on the floor and unlocked it.

All the air whooshed out of Tanya's lungs as Nick flipped on the lights. There, before her, was a series of floor-to-ceiling windows that looked out over Lake

Michigan shimmering with the reflection of the city lights. The apartment itself wasn't half-bad either, but she was so busy looking at the view that she hardly noticed the lap of luxury she'd walked into.

"You...view...wow." She didn't know much about the Chicago housing market—okay, so she knew nothing. Even so, she knew this place had to have cost a fortune—a real, *actual* fortune. Views like that didn't come cheap.

"You like it? It's beautiful at dawn." This statement—which should have been romantic and seductive—was punctuated with another raspberry.

Maybe she'd left reality behind, maybe not. Whether she was dreaming or this was all happening wasn't entirely relevant. Tomorrow would suck, no other way around it, and the days that came after would only get worse and worse.

It didn't matter. Right now, she was in a beautiful place, her baby was happy and Nick was taking care of both of them. She didn't want this moment to end.

When she finally tore her eyes away from the sky and the lake, she was greeted with the sight of Bear riding Nick around a very expensive-looking carpet like a horse. "Giddyap!" Nick said, and then he whinnied. "Come on, pardner, let's show Mommy around!" And he took off down a hall, talking in a thick cowboy accent the whole way.

The image of a high-powered lawyer, who pulled every string he could with doctors and hospitals, galloping around the floor was the funniest thing yet.

She had no idea what was going to happen tomorrow, or the day after that. And even if everything worked out, she couldn't imagine Nick giving up this place for her little house, or even that nice house he was renting. This was what he'd always wanted.

She shook her head, trying to dislodge the what-ifs because they would have to come later. Whatever happened *then* wouldn't take away this moment *now,* where they were a happy family.

Tanya struggled to hold on to that moment in the coming days. There were countless visits with various heads of pediatric this and oncology that. Nick was with her for all the appointments, but after they were over, he'd put Tanya and Bear into a cab and send them back to the apartment so he could go to his office and work on his case. She felt like she never got to see Nick— only Nicholas Long. She didn't think she liked Nicholas Long. He wasn't fun or silly or the least bit tender. In other words, he was the same man who'd shown up on the rez—was that really less than two months ago?— and not the man she'd welcomed back into her bed.

Except at night. For the first few nights, he made passionate love to her in a bed that was as big as her living room. But even that was different—more aggressive, if that was a way to describe sex with Nick. Like he was still trying to prove himself to her.

Then the surgery happened. With the same talk-around-her-in-circles that she was starting to recognize as Nick's true lawyer persona, he convinced her that she shouldn't stay in the hospital with Bear 24/7. "You'll wear yourself out, and what good will you be then?" he'd asked, leading her to yet another cab. "It's like on the airplane, where the flight attendant said to secure your own mask before helping a kid—you've got to secure your own mask."

Which had almost made sense. Then Tanya was back

in the cab—could have been the same one, could have been different, she didn't know—and on her way back to where Darius the doorman was waiting to open her doors for her.

Nick stayed all night, every night with Bear, and then went to his office during the day. Tanya was at the hospital by six-thirty every morning, desperate for good news. Nick had gotten her a cell phone that she couldn't operate, and kept reminding her that no news was good news, but she still arrived at the hospital every morning, convinced that the worst had happened.

It hadn't—not the very worst anyway. The doctors had operated on Bear for over eight hours. The prognosis was good—they got all of the growth. But they had to keep Bear under for a while to give his body time to heal. "Toddlers don't understand IVs," as a nurse had explained it.

So Bear slept. Tanya stayed by his side every day for a week. She sang him songs and rubbed his hands and feet—the only parts of him that didn't have tape and tubes attached. She told him every story she could—how she met his daddy, what had happened to her father, and even Lakota folktales of Iktomi the trickster that she'd thought she had forgotten years ago.

Through it all, she tried to hold on to that happy-family moment. She clung to the thought that after this was all over, they'd go back to being a happy family again.

She was deluding herself, she knew. The more time she spent in Nick's mansion in the sky, the more she realized she'd never be able to hold him. For the last month, Nick had been not just the man of her dreams, but the man she needed—he got the appointments, asked all the right questions and was the rock she leaned on. But she couldn't compete with his place. His life. Nothing she did would ever make Nick forget about the lap of luxury he lived in.

She wanted to think that maybe, just maybe, he'd ask her to come with him again. He'd proven that he could take care of her, after all. And if he was right, and the water was contaminated, wouldn't she be smart to bail? In fact, she'd be stupid to stay on the reservation. It was just land.

Her land, the quiet but insistent voice in the back of her head kept whispering. Her people's land. She didn't know if she would be able to leave the green grass behind to live in a glass tower, with nothing to see but the sky and the water. Assuming Nick even wanted her to come to Chicago with him.

And what about Bear? If Nick didn't stay on the rez, and didn't ask her to come with him to Chicago, then… who would get Bear? Nick could still sue her for custody, and now that she'd seen how he lived, she'd be hard-pressed to argue that Nick couldn't provide for Bear as well as she could. Nick could give their son everything—he'd already gotten him the best medical care possible. Nick could give Bear the best education, food and clothes, all sorts of cultural stuff like plays, concerts, orchestras…

But here, in Chicago, Nick couldn't give Bear the most important culture—his own. Bear wouldn't know he was Lakota if he lived here with Nick. Only Tanya could teach him that, on their homeland.

Tanya tried to shake a little sense back into her head. She was getting ahead of things. She needed to focus on the here and now.

The doctor had come in at ten this morning. He'd said the swelling had gone down, and the scans from yesterday hadn't showed a trace of any growth. "We got it all," the doctor had said, and for the first time, Tanya had seen the man smile. She wished she could remember his name, but that wasn't sticking. The thing that stuck was that he was going to start bringing Bear out of his medically induced coma.

In other words, her son was not only still alive, but he was getting better.

But he hadn't woken up yet. The only things moving in this room were Tanya's hands and Bear's tiny chest. Which was fine—as long as his chest was moving, he could take his time. "You can have all the time you need," Tanya told her baby. "Just keep getting better."

She looked at the clock again. 5:50 p.m. Nick would be here soon. He'd call the nurse in and get all caught up on Bear's progress, then talk with Tanya about their days. After that, he'd call a cab for her and send her back to his huge, empty condo with a kiss and an order to "get some sleep."

She was waiting for Nick in more ways than one. She knew Bear had to come first, but she was surprised by how much she missed Nick—his sharp smiles, the way they fit together, the way he handled everything without even blinking. She didn't like being a shadow he passed in the hall between shifts.

The problem that she couldn't resolve was that as soon as they left this hospital, or as soon as they left Chicago, or as soon as the case was over—at some point, Nick would come back to his super-rich life *here* and she'd go back to her struggling-to-get-by life *there* and Bear would…what? Shuffle between them? Spend half his life on planes?

Then she and Nick would be shadows passing again. Not apart, not like they had been, but not together. And every time she saw him would be like losing him all over again. She might get to have him every so often, but she would never get to hold him.

Struggling once again to remain in the here and now, Tanya waited. She was getting good at it. Waiting for Nick to come. Waiting for Bear to wake up. Waiting to see if he'd still be Bear, or if the surgery had…changed him. Waiting to see if he'd talk, if he could hear.

Her life, on hold.

Nick walked in half an hour later. He was wearing the kind of suit that she guessed lawyers in Chicago wore—a cut-close suit that screamed custom-made. It was a dark gray wool with a faint pinstripe that she wouldn't have thought went with the checked shirt or the striped tie, but somehow worked anyway. He looked dashing, which wasn't a word she'd used in a long time without discussing one-horse open sleighs. His tie had been loosened, and she could see the edges of dark circles under his eyes, but those were the only two signs that he was tired. It wasn't fair, Tanya thought. She knew she probably looked like hell warmed over, and he was still the most handsome man she'd ever seen. Another way they didn't match up.

"Hey, babe." Nick came to her first and kissed her on the forehead. Maybe she was just extra tired, but the gesture almost hurt. What would be left of her and Nick once the Bear emergency was over? Then he went to the other side of Bear's bed and rested his hand on Bear's. "How is he today?"

"Better." Sticking to the facts, she told Nick what the doctor had said about Bear's swelling and coma. "But he hasn't. Woken up yet, that is."

From across the hospital bed, Nick looked at her. For a moment, she saw the high-priced lawyer fall away from his face, and instead, she was sitting across from the boy she'd loved in high school—the one who'd talked about all the things he'd buy her when they grew up. "He will wake up, Tanya. You've got to believe that." Just then his cell phone buzzed. He looked at the screen, grimaced and said, "Sorry, I've got to take this," before he went out into the hall.

She didn't mean to listen, but the room was silent except for the beeping of the machines, which left plenty of space for Nick's low, serious voice to carry.

"No—*no.* Absolutely not." He was silent for a moment, then, in an even lower voice, said, "I don't care what you want—and crying won't work. I'm busy."

Tanya's heart did a swan dive. That didn't sound like a business conversation. That sounded like a personal conversation—a *very* personal conversation.

Things had happened so quickly. She and Nick had just started to reconnect when Bear's illness had taken over their lives. There hadn't been time to really discuss a future outside of this hospital room. Tanya had never even found out if he had been involved with someone— if he was *still* involved with someone. She'd assumed— believed—that Nick wouldn't two-time anyone. He wasn't that kind of man.

But she realized that she might have been wrong. The old Nick, the one who took her on joyrides in the middle of the night—he wouldn't cheat on her, much less on anyone else. But the new Nick? The one who owned lakefront condos? The one who wore custom-made suits and won major lawsuits? The one who decided things for her without telling her?

She didn't know what this Nick would do.

You're being ridiculous, she scolded herself. *You shouldn't jump to conclusions right now—you'll jump right off a cliff.* Nick was here with her and Bear because they were important to him. Whoever was on that phone wasn't winning his or her argument, because Nick was busy with Tanya and Bear. He was here. That's all that mattered right now.

She forced herself to start humming so she wouldn't listen to the rest of Nick's conversation. The fact that she was even worried about another woman was probably just an indicator of how deeply tired she was. Getting worked up over what was probably nothing didn't do anyone any good—least of all her. She took a deep breath, attempting to regain her calm. Whatever the problem was, they could deal with it when the time was right. That's what she had to remember.

When Nick came back into the room, he was shaking his head. "Is everything okay?" she asked, trying to keep her tone light. She didn't want him to think she'd been eavesdropping.

He flopped down into the chair and ran a hand through his hair while he looked at her. Tanya began to squirm under his gaze—there was something intense about the way he was staring at her, and that intensity made her uncomfortable. "Tanya," he began, his tone serious.

Her heart dropped down another notch. Was this about that phone call, or was it something else Nick had "decided" for her? She'd meant to have a discussion with him about his doing things without telling her, but that conversation had gotten lost in the urgency of the past few weeks. Maybe this was just the precursor to the end. She knew she couldn't hold him. The sooner they both acknowledged that fact, the less pain there'd be in the end. She steeled herself for the conversation she'd been dreading. "Yes?"

She didn't get it. After another long look loaded with meaning she couldn't interpret, Nick half spoke, half mumbled, "You look tired. Go home, get some sleep. I'll call you a cab."

She felt like she should press him—she shouldn't let him off the hook. But what did she know? Not much beyond the facts. And the facts were, it was late and she was exhausted. If she hounded him on that call, she'd look insecure at best, and at worst? Well, she didn't want to push Nick any further than necessary. Maybe tonight, she'd sleep. Then tomorrow she could try to figure out what was going on. That was the best plan.

"Daddy's here," she told Bear as she kissed his hand good-night. "I'll see you in the morning, okay, sweetie? I love you."

Nick walked her out to the hall. "He's going to be fine," he said again. Then he kissed her with more force than she'd come to expect from their little evening ritual. She wanted to get lost in him, if only to forget being worried and tired and scared. When he pulled away, he rested his forehead against hers and said, "Everything is going to be fine."

This time, Tanya wasn't sure if he was trying to convince her or himself.

Tanya would say this: she was, well, maybe not getting used to the cab ride and the insane amount of traffic and the sheer noise of going from the north side of the city to Nick's condo. But she was less terrified by the whole thing, so that had to count for something.

"Evening, Ms. Rattling Blanket."

Tanya looked up, expecting to see Darius the doorman again. Except it wasn't—it was someone she'd never seen before. That he knew who she was made her nervous. "Hello."

The doorman tipped his hat as he held the door for her, which made Tanya feel weird. Was she supposed to be giving him money for that? Or not? She nodded and smiled and said, "Thank you," as she hurried in.

Once inside the elevator, she punched in Nick's floor—thirty-first. The ride up was another thing she was getting used to.

The hallway was silent, but something had the hackles rising on the back of her neck. Nothing looked out of place. But her level of paranoia wasn't healthy. Maybe a glass of beer or wine in Nick's expensive-looking bar would let her sleep.

She unlocked Nick's door, and instantly she knew she wasn't being paranoid at all. Music filled his apartment, competing with a weird mix of lavender and... garlic? Who broke into someone's apartment to cook?

Something wasn't right. Before Tanya could back out and get the doorman, a flirty feminine voice called out, "Nicky? Is that you?"

Nicky? Nick hated that name. He'd settle for Nicholas when he had to, but Tanya had several clear memories of him brawling with guys in high school because they'd call him Nicky just to piss him off.

Then the body to match that voice came around the corner. *Tall* was the first thing Tanya thought, followed closely by *blonde*. *Skin* was third because this woman certainly was showing a lot of it. She had on a lacy apron and not much else—maybe just a bra and panties. And heels. Who the hell cooked in heels?

"Nicky, I—" The nearly naked woman pulled up short when she saw Tanya. She crossed her arms in front of her chest. "You're not Nicky."

Thoughts crashed around Tanya like cymbals in a parade. This wasn't a break-in—this woman had a key. She was probably the person Nick had been talking to on the phone. He had dated her—might still be with her, for all Tanya knew. And she was, for lack of a better term, hot. Gorgeous.

Another reason for her to believe she'd never be able to hold Nick. Not when he had a woman like this parading around this place in her underwear.

But that's not what came out. Instead, Tanya said, "Who are you?" which wasn't the most brilliant statement ever, but it was all she had.

"Who am I?" For a woman wearing next to nothing, she managed to pull off a surprisingly indignant tone of voice, like she couldn't believe that Tanya didn't recognize her. "I'm Clarissa Sutcliffe. Of the Chicago Sutcliffes. If you're the maid, you can come back tomorrow."

Oh—the *Chicago* Sutcliffes. Of course, Tanya wanted to say. She managed to keep that retort in, but not by much. "I'm not a maid."

Where had she heard the name Sutcliffe? Oh. Oh, *no*. Sutcliffe—as in Sutcliffe, Watkins and Monroe. As in Nick's boss.

He'd been screwing the boss's daughter.

Clarissa Sutcliffe unfolded her arms and struck what could only be described as a supermodel pose—feet shoulder-width apart, hip popped out, chest puffed up. Damn, she had a hell of a body—one that Tanya would never be able to get close to. The worst part was, they both knew it. "Oh, that's right. Daddy said Nicky had brought some Indian people into town for the case he was working on. I didn't realize he was letting a witness stay with him."

Tanya's brain exploded with everything that was wrong with those statements. Some Indian people? A witness? Letting her stay here? Where the hell else would she stay? Any thoughts of being polite went out the window. "Don't you need to put on some pants, or do you usually walk around in your underwear?"

She shouldn't have said that because whatever Clarissa Sutcliffe was, she had Tanya beat in the "bitch" category, hands down. She took her sweet time giving Tanya the once-over, which had the weird effect of making Tanya feel like she was the naked one in the room. The whole time, her mind spun in wild circles around two words—Nick's witness.

He was going to use Bear. He was going to put her on the stand. Her whole life would be dragged into court. The other lawyers—they'd cut her to shreds. Everyone would think she was a terrible mother.

Nick had lied to her.

This Clarissa shook her head, a gesture of mock pity and condescending disapproval. "He's mine, you know. It's *adorable* that you think he's in love with you, but when he's done with…" she waved her hand in Tanya's general direction "…you, he'll come back to me." She rolled her shoulder, a move that would have come off as seductive if it hadn't been so mercenary. "He knows which one of us is the smart money."

A wave of nausea piled on to Tanya's confusion. This Clarissa was right, of course. Money—and power—were what Nick wanted, more than he wanted her. Tanya had always known that, but the confirmation sucked more than she'd thought it would.

"Do you know where he is?" she asked Clarissa. She wasn't about to go down without a fight, damn it. She had weapons at her disposal—facts. "Do you have any idea where he's at *right now?* Or last night? Or the night before?"

Finally, she saw a crack in Clarissa's supreme confidence. "I—" But whatever she was going to say tripped her up. She just glared at Tanya instead.

"He's at Children's Hospital." The facts—that's what Tanya had. And she was going to use them, by God. "He's keeping a bedside vigil over his son—*our* son. Our one-year-old son who has brain cancer." Clarissa took a step back, then two, in shock. That's right, Tanya thought. Just the facts. "He won't come back here tonight. He won't be back tomorrow night. So if you're arranging any other surprises, you might want to reconsider those plans." Now it was her turn to wave her hand in dismissal. "*All* of them."

Which was ridiculous. She had absolutely no control over what Nick would do next. But right now, she wanted to make sure this woman didn't think she could walk all over Tanya just because she was poor and Indian and didn't dress or look like a lingerie model.

"He has a *son?*" Clarissa looked truly horrified. "With *you?*"

That did it. Tanya was too exhausted and worried about Bear to stand here and be cut to shreds by a socialite playing chef. Tanya took three quick steps forward, the lavender smell getting stronger with each step. Clarissa fell back so fast that she lost one of her heels and almost toppled over. That was satisfying enough, but one other thing bothered Tanya. "You want to say that again?"

Tanya must have looked like she was about to clock Clarissa something good because any trace of superiority was gone, replaced by a look of sheer terror. Clarissa lost her other shoe, then retreated to where some clothes were spread out on a couch. "He told my father you were a witness! He said you were here for his case!" She scooped up her things and gave Tanya a wide berth. "He never said he had a son."

Then she was gone in a swirl of floral perfume.

Tanya stood there in a state of shock. Nick was building his case on his own son's health, even though he knew she didn't want Bear involved. All because he wanted to win. He was going to put her on the stand, where the bad guys would have plenty of chance to make her look like the world's worst mother. And to heap insult on to injury, he'd done all of this without as much as a whisper about his plans to her.

Because she wasn't a part of his plans.

The truth hurt worse than she'd thought possible.

Fourteen

As he'd done for the last week, Nick pulled Bear's copy of *The Very Hungry Caterpillar* out of his bag. "I have some new stories," he told his son. "My secretary brought in a few that she said her kids loved. But we'll start with your favorite, okay?"

He settled down in the chair, keeping one hand on Bear's chest. He felt better having that firsthand knowledge of Bear's continual breathing.

He opened the book and started reading. By this point, he didn't actually have to look at the words. He had this story down cold. As he went through the book, his mind rehashed the day.

And what a day it had been. Marcus had called him in for a briefing first thing this morning. Nick was all but mainlining coffee at this point, but he hadn't been quite as sharp as he'd needed to be. After they'd gone over the state of Nick's case, Marcus had said, "You haven't been by to see Rissa yet, son," in a tone of voice that should have set off every single warning bell in Nick's head but hadn't.

"I've been busy." It was only after that pat answer had hung in the air for a few moments that Nick had realized how thin the ice he was treading upon really was. "This case has been taking up a lot of my time," he added, but that excuse had sounded plenty weak.

"Is everything okay between you two? I'd expected you to get engaged before you took this case." Marcus had started shuffling papers around on his desk, but now that he was fully awake, Nick wasn't going to let that casual activity distract him.

No doubt Rissa had expected the same thing. He'd been gone for two months and had apparently forgotten how to play the game in that short amount of time. Either that, or the game had become much less important. "We're fine."

Marcus had steepled his fingers together, looking like a cartoon caricature of a boss. "I know that these are your people, Nicholas, but I'm worried that you may be in over your head on this case. I'm thinking of asking Jenkins to join you. Just to help out."

That had been a demotion, plain and simple—a vote of little-to-no confidence. Maybe Marcus no longer felt like he had Nick completely under his thumb; maybe Rissa had planted a whole garden of doubt. Maybe it was just that Marcus had remembered how much of an Indian Nick really was. Whatever the reason, Nick was on his way down.

The odd thing was, he hadn't really cared. For once, it wasn't his career that pushed him. For perhaps the first time in his life, it was justice. "I'll see this case through to the end, one way or another," was all he had said. No grand posturing, no veiled threats. He wasn't playing the game anymore.

And then that call from Rissa. Like her crocodile tears would have swayed him now. There would have been a time when he might have let that work—it had been easier to keep her happy than to provoke her—but not any longer. Talking to her again was just another reminder of how much he had to get away from the life he'd made here. How had these people become his definition of success? How had he let himself get drawn into a world of emotional manipulation?

Tanya had shown him another way—a way to be happy, with her and with Bear. Maybe he'd just needed to hear Rissa's voice to realize how life with her would always be a game of lies and deceit—in stark contrast to how honest, how real, Tanya was. How much he needed her, like he needed the wide-open sky and the smell of the prairie after a hard rain. With Tanya, what he saw was what he got.

They had a future together. For the first time, he considered a future that didn't involve the law firm of Sutcliffe, Watkins and Monroe, a future that didn't involve Chicago. He *would* see this case to the end—of that, he had no doubt. But he didn't have to be tied to the Sutcliffes to make it in the world, not anymore.

As soon as he and Tanya had weathered this storm together, they needed to sit down and figure out how to make things work, starting with getting married. He could buy that house, or he could build her one a little closer to the rez. Emily Mankiller would hire him outright to see the case through, and after that, he'd start his own high-powered environmental law firm. There was a whole world of possibilities out there—a whole life of his own making, just waiting for him.

But right now, he had bigger things to worry about. Like the little boy in the bed next to him, his chest rising and falling in a steady beat. Nick could feel Bear's tiny heartbeat under his skin. The rhythm was strong, like the drumbeat at the powwow.

He leaned down, resting his head next to Bear's on the bed. The smell was both the familiar scent of his son and the sterile antiseptic of hospital bandages. He couldn't wait to get the boy out of here.

"I know you're going to be fine. I can feel it here," he said, patting Bear's chest. This was as close to holding the boy as he could get with all the tubes and wires. He knew he had already done everything within his power for his son, but it didn't feel like enough. Despite his wealth and his track record in the courtroom, he couldn't fix this. He couldn't make Bear wake up.

He forced himself to stay positive. Kids fed off of positive energy—one of the nurses who had come and gone in the last week had said that. "You're going to grow up to be a man with a voice—a strong warrior that makes us proud. But you've got to wake up first," he went on, feeling the catch in his throat. "Your mommy is worried about you, you know. She's scared…" He paused, clearing his throat. He was scared, too, and he hated that feeling. He'd give up everything—the fancy car, the condo, the perks of power—all of it, in exchange for his son being okay.

He had to stay positive. "So let's make her feel better, okay? Let's make Mommy happy. All you have to do is wake up, Bear."

And then, because even though Bear was still unconscious, his pulse was beating out a steady rhythm, Nick began to sing. Not the nursery rhymes that Tanya sang, but the song of the powwow. Songs Nick hadn't sang in years—decades—came back to him. He felt the "Honored Warrior" song raise itself from some forgotten part of his memory, the words shaking the dust off themselves to flow from his mouth. He didn't know the words in Lakota, but he remembered the English version.

"They have made a brave warrior," he sang, his voice soft but keeping time with Bear's heartbeat, "from this Lakota boy. They are walking with him."

He sang those words over and over, feeling the power of the beat. The song wasn't a prayer; it was a promise, carried from the past through the present, to the future. This was his promise to his son. He would honor his promise, come hell or high water.

He finished one refrain and was about to start again when he heard a noise. When he lifted his head, he saw Tanya standing in the doorway.

For a fraction of a second, he was happy to see her, happy that she'd come. But that fraction of happiness was all he got.

Her eyes flashed with a rage that any fool would be afraid of, and Nick liked to think he was no fool. He could see her hands were clenched into fists, and her chest heaved with angry breaths.

Hell.

"When were you going to tell me, Nick?" She kept her voice low, but there was no mistaking the danger in her tone. "Were you *ever* going to tell me?"

Rissa. That was all he knew for sure. Part of his brain scrambled for damage control—but the problem was, he didn't know exactly what kind of damage he was trying to control. "Babe..."

"Don't you 'babe' me. Don't you *dare*." She advanced on him, her arms swinging low. She wouldn't punch him in a hospital, would she? He scrambled to his feet and took a precautionary step away from her. The only place to go was on the other side of Bear's bed. "Why did you do it?"

It probably wouldn't help his point to ask which "it" she was referring to. He decided to stick with the least incriminating. "Rissa and I agreed to see other people before I left. I hadn't even talked to her before today."

He expected more fury from her, but the wash of sadness caught him off guard. As quick as it had come, though, it was gone. "You think this is about that—that—*her?* Oh, for God's sake." She threw up her hands and spun on her heels, which had the convenient side effect of taking her out of swinging range. "This is about the case, Nick. Your case. The one where you're going to use my son as your first—hell, maybe your only— piece of evidence. When were you going to tell me about *that,* huh? When you called me to the freaking stand?"

Rare had been the day when Nick had met a situation he couldn't talk himself out of. Hell, that's all that being a lawyer really was—being able to talk your way out of whatever trap the opposition laid for you.

But this was different. Maybe it was the lost nights of sleep, maybe it was that Tanya hadn't laid him in a trap at all—more like she'd caught him in his own. Whatever the reason, he wasn't talking his way out of this one.

"I was going to discuss it with you." Even as he said it, he knew it would help nothing.

"Are you serious? You let me sit here for days— weeks—thinking that you listened to me when I told you I didn't want Bear to be a part of this. And did that matter to you? No. You don't care about me, you don't even care about our son. You only care about two things, Nick—you and your stupid case."

What could he do? Denial was pointless—she had him dead to rights. In any other situation, he would have told her so. His only hope was to make her see his side. "Tanya, I have a legal obligation to my client—"

She whirled around. "Seriously? You're going to throw that out there?" Something in her face softened. She knew he was right. But she wasn't done with him yet. "Yet another choice you made for me, instead of with me. And what about your legal obligation to your family? What about your obligation to me?" Her voice caught, and he saw the tears she was fighting so hard to keep in. "Why did you make me think you cared for me if all you wanted was to use Bear as evidence? You didn't have to break my heart again, Nick. That was just cruel."

To hell with this. He crossed the space between them, grabbed her arm and spun her around until they were face-to-face. "I did no such thing, and you know it. I love you—I always have. You're the only person who makes me feel like an actual person—not some object of pity, not some token of affirmative action. You make me real, Tanya. I lost that for too long, but coming home again..." The tears spilled over now, cutting glistening paths down her cheeks. He cupped her face and wiped them away with his thumbs. "This isn't how I planned to tell you, but I'm not going to let you go without a fight. I want us to work this time, Tanya. I want to make a life with you—here or there, it doesn't matter to me anymore because I see now that my home is wherever you are."

"How can I believe you?" Her voice broke, but she didn't let that stop her. "How can I trust you, Nick? How do I know that there won't be other fancy women in their underwear, waiting to make you dinner?"

Oh, *hell*. He could see it now—Rissa waiting for him to come back to the condo, and having a drama queen–sized hissy fit when Tanya innocently walked in. Obviously, Marcus hadn't bothered to maintain the same level of confidentiality that Nick did.

"She told you about the case?" He knew he was risking another outburst, but he had to make sure he had everything right. He didn't want to fly off the handle with incomplete information.

Tanya nodded. More tears. But unlike Rissa, Nick knew these weren't designed to get her way—these were real. "She said…you'd go back to her. You knew which one was the smart money."

"Someone once told me something important—'I don't need all that stuff, not as long as I've got you.'" She gasped a little when he said it. That had been what Tanya had always told him, back when he was too young and impulsive to really hear what she was saying. He knew better now. "I only wish I'd listened then, because you know what? I will pick the smart woman over the smart money every day of the week."

She stared at him, a few errant tears escaping. He could see her confusion as she tried to figure out if she should trust him or not. "But the case…"

"Tanya, I was going to talk to you about it—not to trap you, not to trick you and not to make you do anything you didn't want. But you've got to look at the bigger picture here. Midwest Energy destroyed our land—the land you've worked so hard to keep. They're hurting our people—not just Bear, not just your mother, but *our* people." The words felt freeing as he said them. He realized that while he'd been counting Tanya and Bear as "his," he hadn't made that final leap to the entire tribe. But for all of his jerky racism, Marcus Sutcliffe

was right. The Red Creek Lakota were Nick's people—
and he would fight for them, first and foremost. "You've
worked so hard for the tribe, for Emily—you can't turn
your back on that just because you're afraid of some
lawyer's dirty tricks. That doesn't help Bear, and that
doesn't help our people."

The tears flowed a little heavier. "You—you know
I'm not a bad mother, though, right?"

"Oh, babe." He couldn't help but laugh at that statement as he pulled her into a hug. "Even if the defense
attorneys tried to paint you as a terrible mother, you
think I don't have a few tricks of my own up my sleeve?
You think I wouldn't come back at them with guns blazing? You think I'd let someone slander you in public
and walk away in one piece?" He kissed her forehead.
"Not a chance. I'm going to fight for you—both of you.
You're not only not a bad mother, you're the best mother
I could want my son to have."

She gasped in surprise. Was it possible that she'd
spent all this time thinking she wasn't good enough? "I
want to believe you this time, Nick. I really do. But…"

Boy, had he earned that hit. Despite himself, he felt
a smile twitch at the corner of his mouth. "May I as-
sume you told Rissa about Bear?"

"You mean Clarissa Sutcliffe, of the Chicago Sutcliffes?" She snorted in derision. "I suppose I should
be comforted by the fact that she had no idea you had
a son. I'm not the only person you hold out on. When
were you going to tell me about *that?*"

Nick was so thrilled to hear the note—however
faint—of teasing in her voice that he had to resist the
urge to laugh. "Because the relationship had ended, I
didn't think rehashing it with you was the best course
of action." Tanya shot him a look that said, quite clearly,

Oh, come on. "It's true. The relationship was over before I left Chicago, and then you and I…well, finding you again put anything to do with the Chicago Sutcliffes far from my mind."

"But her dad—he's your boss, right?"

"Tanya, I swear that, from this point on, I will consult you early and often. You have my word." He cleared his throat. This was it—he was all in. "So, I'm thinking about quitting my job, but I'd like to get your input on that decision."

She gasped again. Too much more of this and she'd be in danger of hyperventilating. "You *what?* But your case! You have a life here!"

He traced the curve of her cheek again. "I am not giving up on this case. I can work for the tribe directly. And I have a life, all right—but it's not here. My life is with you and Bear, Tanya. My life is out on our land. Or near it. I could always buy that house. It's only an hour away from the rez. Or we could get something closer, but that's still, you know…"

"Nice. Nicer than what we had growing up." More tears, but this time, she was grinning through them. "Like we always talked about."

"Like I promised you," he agreed. "But I'd want to get married—I don't want what we have to slip away again because of misunderstandings." Her mouth hung open in sheer shock. He couldn't tell if that was a good thing or not. She was kind of freaking him out. Heck, this whole conversation was kind of freaking him out. He'd been so wrapped up in Bear's surgery and his case that he hadn't spent a whole lot of time thinking about what came next. But it felt right—more right than anything had felt in a long, long time. "Will you marry me? I can't lose you again."

"Oh, Nick, you mean that?"

"I love you. No matter what happens, I'm not going anywhere. And that's a promise I will keep until my dying day, babe." Then, finally, he kissed her.

She threw herself into the embrace, which he took as a *yes*. The kiss deepened—he'd missed her so much these last few days—but then the weirdest noise came from behind them. It was small and almost mewing, like a kitten crying out for the very first time.

Tanya jerked out of his arms. "Did you hear *that?*" Hope burned in her eyes.

He nodded, afraid to hope. They both turned to the bed where their son lay.

Bear's head moved—just a little—his mouth opened, and the noise came out of it again. Small, yes. But a sound, nonetheless.

"Bear!"

Tanya rushed to the boy while Nick all but threw himself out the door, hollering for every available nurse, "He's awake! He's trying to cry!" Then he hurried back to Tanya's side. Holding hands, they listened together as their son made his first sounds.

Somehow, it just felt right.

Epilogue

Nick pulled into the driveway of his house and sat, enjoying the last few minutes of silence as he mentally packed away the day in court and geared up for the long night ahead. He liked this house. They'd lived in the rental while this one was built on the edge of the rez. Tanya had wanted something that wasn't hers or his, but theirs, so he'd hired an architect and let her go crazy. The only things he'd demanded were a master suite, a home office and a four-car garage. Between the long winter months and the child seats, he didn't get to drive his Jag as much these days. However, he wasn't about to sell that car. It had a place of honor, next to the family SUV and his truck.

Mentally, he was already thinking about what the fourth car would be—*after* he won his case and got paid out of the settlement. Midwest Energy was on the ropes, and everyone knew it. Their lead lawyer had asked for a meeting first thing tomorrow morning. Nick knew a settlement offer was headed his way—but he also knew it would be a pitiful, lowball offer and that he was going to do everything but throw it back in their face.

Midwest was going to pay for the cleanup and the extensive medical bills their pollution had generated, that much was certain. After Tanya's testimony—two days of her being the calm, reliable witness he'd always known she would be, combined with the photos of Bear coming out of his surgery wrapped in tubes and wires—Midwest knew they had lost the battle and the war wasn't far behind. It was their call—they could pay for it voluntarily, or they could wait until the jury handed the Red Creek Lakota one of the biggest financial rewards in the country. Either way, Nick would make them pay.

The case had taken up years of his life, but he hadn't minded. He worked for Emily Mankiller directly now, and she was a more engaging boss than Marcus Sutcliffe had ever been. He'd gotten comfortable being on the rez again. In fact, Emily had asked him to stay on after the case as the lawyer for the tribe, but Nick wasn't a tribal law specialist. He wanted his own environmentalist firm. He had a feeling that a lot of people—Lakota and non-Lakota—were watching this court case. He suspected he'd have more cases than he could handle once the verdict was in, but he wouldn't have to bow and scrape to anyone. He'd be his own boss. Even though he missed a doorman on those days when he had to get out the snowblower and clean off his own drive, he still wouldn't trade this life for his old one.

He saw the curtains move and Doreen's face peek out. She'd been staying at the house to help out Tanya while Nick was in the final leg of his case, but she had what Tanya had declared was a "hot date" tonight. Nick tried not to think about what that entailed, and instead focused on the fact that his mother-in-law was healthy enough to help out around the house *and* enjoy an active social life. Not bad for someone who'd been having strokes for a year.

Nick grabbed his laptop and headed into the house. "I'm home," he announced. "Everybody still pregnant?" was all he got out before the ball of energy that was his son came barreling down the stairs.

"DADDY!" Bear, now three, tackled him hard and low, just at the knees. It took everything Nick had to keep his footing. "Daddy, you're home! I had the most funnest day ever with Nana! She took me to the store and let me pick out my very own apples—you and Mommy can't have them, but Nana got some for you to share. But you can't have my apples, 'cause they're mine, okay?"

Nick swooped his son up into his arms. "Slow down there, little guy. Something about apples, you say?"

"Daddy!" Bear did his best interpretation of Tanya being frustrated. "You're not listening to me!"

Nick smiled and hugged his son. "Yes, I am, Bear." The boy squirmed out of Nick's arms and was gone in a flash, announcing Nick's arrival to his Nana. Some days the verbal barrage was overwhelming, but on those days, all Nick had to do was think back to the silent little boy he'd first met. He'd take all the talking, every day of the week.

Tanya popped her head out from the kitchen, followed shortly by her enormous belly. "Oh, thank heavens."

Standing behind his wife, he reached around and patted her belly. "How's my baby girl today?"

"Active." Tanya leaned back into him. Nick savored the feeling of her against him. He'd missed everything the first time, but nothing—not even the biggest case of his career—would keep him from Tanya's side this time. "Bear is all yours tonight, by the way."

"I'd rather be all yours, babe." She smiled as she arched back to kiss him on the cheek. He cupped her belly, feeling the whole thing jump with each active kick. Somehow, it just felt right.

He wouldn't have it any other way.

* * * * *

REQUEST YOUR FREE BOOKS!

2 FREE NOVELS PLUS 2 FREE GIFTS!

Harlequin®

Desire

ALWAYS POWERFUL, PASSIONATE AND PROVOCATIVE

YES! Please send me 2 FREE Harlequin Desire® novels and my 2 FREE gifts (gifts are worth about $10). After receiving them, if I don't wish to receive any more books, I can return the shipping statement marked "cancel." If I don't cancel, I will receive 6 brand-new novels every month and be billed just $4.30 per book in the U.S. or $4.99 per book in Canada. That's a saving of at least 14% off the cover price! It's quite a bargain! Shipping and handling is just 50¢ per book in the U.S. and 75¢ per book in Canada.* I understand that accepting the 2 free books and gifts places me under no obligation to buy anything. I can always return a shipment and cancel at any time. Even if I never buy another book, the two free books and gifts are mine to keep forever.

225/326 HDN FEF3

Name _____ (PLEASE PRINT) _____

Address _____ Apt. #

City _____ State/Prov. _____ Zip/Postal Code

Signature (if under 18, a parent or guardian must sign)

Mail to the **Reader Service:**
IN U.S.A.: P.O. Box 1867, Buffalo, NY 14240-1867
IN CANADA: P.O. Box 609, Fort Erie, Ontario L2A 5X3

Not valid for current subscribers to Harlequin Desire books.

Want to try two free books from another line?
Call 1-800-873-8635 or visit www.ReaderService.com.

* Terms and prices subject to change without notice. Prices do not include applicable taxes. Sales tax applicable in N.Y. Canadian residents will be charged applicable taxes. Offer not valid in Quebec. This offer is limited to one order per household. All orders subject to credit approval. Credit or debit balances in a customer's account(s) may be offset by any other outstanding balance owed by or to the customer. Please allow 4 to 6 weeks for delivery. Offer available while quantities last.

Your Privacy—The Reader Service is committed to protecting your privacy. Our Privacy Policy is available online at www.ReaderService.com or upon request from the Reader Service.

We make a portion of our mailing list available to reputable third parties that offer products we believe may interest you. If you prefer that we not exchange your name with third parties, or if you wish to clarify or modify your communication preferences, please visit us at www.ReaderService.com/consumerchoice or write to us at Reader Service Preference Service, P.O. Box 9062, Buffalo, NY 14269. Include your complete name and address.

HDES11B

New York Times *bestselling author Brenda Jackson
presents TEXAS WILD,
a brand-new Westmoreland novel.*

Available October 2012 from Harlequin Desire®!

Rico figured there were a lot of things in life he didn't know. But the one thing he did know was that there was no way Megan Westmoreland was going to Texas with him. He was attracted to her, big-time, and had been from the moment he'd seen her at Micah's wedding four months ago. Being alone with her in her office was bad enough. But the idea of them sitting together on a plane or in a car was arousing him just thinking about it.

He could tell by the mutinous expression on her face that he was in for a fight. That didn't bother him. Growing up, he'd had two younger sisters to deal with, so he knew well how to handle a stubborn female.

She crossed her arms over her chest. "Other than the fact that you prefer working alone, give me another reason I can't go with you."

He crossed his arms over his own chest. "I don't need another reason. You and I talked before I took this case, and I told you I would get you the information you wanted… doing things my way."

He watched as she nibbled on her bottom lip. So now she was remembering. Good. Even so, he couldn't stop looking into her beautiful dark eyes, meeting her fiery gaze head-on.

"As the client, I demand that you take me," she said.

He narrowed his gaze. "You can demand all you want, but you're not going to Texas with me."

Megan's jaw dropped. "I *will* be going with you since there's no good reason that I shouldn't."

He didn't say anything for a moment. "Okay, there is another reason I won't take you with me. One that you'd do well to consider," he said in a barely controlled tone. She had pushed him, and he didn't like being pushed.

"Fine, let's hear it," she snapped furiously.

He placed his hands in the pockets of his jeans, stood with his legs braced apart and leveled his gaze on her. "I want you, Megan. Bad. And if you go anywhere with me, I'm going to have you."

He then turned and walked out of her office.

Will Megan go to Texas with Rico?

Find out in Brenda Jackson's brand-new Westmoreland novel, TEXAS WILD.

Available October 2012 from Harlequin Desire®.

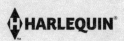